Xathi

Daybook of

ALLAN STEELE

7:00 a.m.	Work out at gym
8:00 a.m.	_COFFEE!!_
8:10 a.m.	Meeting with Grady
9:00 a.m.	Check stock market
9:15 a.m.	Meeting with Clyde Simmington
10:00 a.m.	Leave for Vermont—_directions???_
3:00 p.m.	WEDDING TO JANE
4:00 p.m.	Wedding cake
5:00 p.m.	Check stock market closing

FALL IN LOVE!

Zelda the Cow

ABOUT THE AUTHOR

Ever since she can remember, Liz Ireland
has been a fan of screwball comedies. So in
Allan Steele, she savored the chance to create the
most fanciful of heroes—a dyed-in-the-wool
curmudgeon who by happy accident gets a second
chance at love. She hopes amnesiac Allan is a
hero readers can't forget!

Liz lives in Austin, Texas, where she loves to
swim, read, watch movies and care for a houseful
of pets.

Books by Liz Ireland

HARLEQUIN AMERICAN ROMANCE
639—HEAVEN-SENT HUSBAND

HARLEQUIN HISTORICALS
286—CECILIA AND THE STRANGER
330—MILLIE AND THE FUGITIVE

Don't miss any of our special offers. Write to us at the
following address for information on our newest releases.

Harlequin Reader Service
U.S.: 3010 Walden Ave., P.O. Box 1325, Buffalo, NY 14269
Canadian: P.O. Box 609, Fort Erie, Ont. L2A 5X3

Liz Ireland

THE GROOM FORGETS

Harlequin Books

TORONTO • NEW YORK • LONDON
AMSTERDAM • PARIS • SYDNEY • HAMBURG
STOCKHOLM • ATHENS • TOKYO • MILAN
MADRID • WARSAW • BUDAPEST • AUCKLAND

ISBN 0-373-16683-4

THE GROOM FORGETS

Copyright © 1997 by Elizabeth Bass

Prologue

Vermont! Allan Steele thought peevishly. Who would have ever guessed that *he* would be getting married in Vermont?

The silver-gray Mercedes convertible with a black top sped furiously up and down the gently swelling hills of the two-lane, curvy road. The day was drizzly and uncomfortably cool, one of those early spring chills that could make a person nostalgic for the dog days of August.

Allan breathed out a long exasperated stream of cigarette smoke and hit the gas as he topped the crest of a hill. Well, at least after today this wedding would be over with. His bachelor days would finally be behind him, he and Jane would settle down into a serviceable routine, and he could forget all about personal problems and concentrate on what interested him most: making money.

Best of all, after this damn wedding he would probably never think of Patricia Blakemore.

That's right, he grumbled cynically to himself. Life would be just hunky-dory—after the wedding. But it was raining, and he was lost, and there wouldn't be a wedding if he couldn't find the blasted farm Jane's father owned.

Vermont? Until two days ago he hadn't even known Jane came from Vermont! The five years she'd been his right-hand man at Steele and Grimly, Jane had lived in Brooklyn, so when they agreed to marry, he'd assumed they'd just jump in a cab and go to city hall. He never dreamed that sensible Jane would want a private ceremony, or that he'd have to take two whole days off from work, drive out all this way and get married among a lot of cows and bugs and relatives.

Women, he thought disgustedly, taking a staccato drag on his high-nicotine, high-tar, high-priced imported cigarette. Women were forever keeping their little secrets and springing them on a guy when he was least able to stick up for himself. He couldn't very well have told Jane to forget the bucolic wedding thing without sounding like a complete pill.

Which reminded him—his head was splitting. He reached over, flipped open the glove compartment and rooted around with his hand until he found a little bottle of antihistamines. Clean country air always made him sick. He popped two pills, washed them down with a swig of flat diet soda and lit another smoke.

Vermont! He liked New York City, a place with grit, a place with a pulse all its own. Everything here seemed too green, too annoyingly pure.

A four-way intersection loomed ahead and he slammed on the brakes. That farm had to be around here somewhere. Jane had drawn him a map, but he'd lost track of what those stupid road signs were telling him miles ago. He'd have to call her for more directions. Meanwhile, he'd turn right.

The pristine treads on his tires sent gravel and mud

spewing in his wake as he accelerated. God, he loved his car, loved it so much he almost cracked a smile.

Instead, he picked up the phone and, keeping half an eye on the road, punched in the number Jane had written in her clear handwriting at the bottom of the map. Great girl, Jane. Very tall—nice legs. Efficient, too. He wouldn't regret marrying her. Especially not if the single night they had spent together was any indication of what their married relationship would be....

His ear was greeted with something it hadn't heard in so long that his brain actually had a hard time computing the sound. *A busy signal!* Jane's father didn't have Call Waiting?

He slammed the phone down in its cradle and sucked on his cigarette to calm his nerves. He hated it when things didn't go his way. And now he was late, late, late. Jane would expect that, of course, having worked with him for years. Still, it *was* his wedding day.

Drumming his fingers on the dash, he considered his options. That was one of his mottoes: Always keep an eye on your options. Life wasn't so different from business. In either, a person could plunge ahead, freeze or bail out. He was already plunging ahead and freezing, so that left bailing out.

He wondered briefly what would happen if he turned tail and drove back to New York City—if he could manage to find it. Jane's family would be outraged, but it would all blow over in the end. He would give Jane a few days off, let her rest up in the country. It would crush her, of course, but she would get over him eventually. He wouldn't be the first groom to skip out on a woman.

Brides certainly did it often enough to men! He knew that from bitter experience. He had only been two weeks away from the altar when Patricia ran off to Paris, having decided, apparently, that a liaison with the most powerful man in network television would further her news career faster than marriage to a mere multimillionaire stockbroker.

He couldn't fault anyone for wanting to get ahead. Not for nothing had *The Wall Street Journal* dubbed him "the barracuda of Wall Street." Maybe that was just his problem. Maybe he was too cynical and ruthless.

Except when it came to Patricia Blakemore. She was everything he ever wanted—tall, beautiful, successful and from a rich family. *If I could just have Patricia,* he used to think to himself, *I would be able to relax.* Then he would know he'd arrived in the world of rich untouchables. Forgotten would be the hungry days of his youth, and the bitterness he'd built up through the years. Maybe he'd even get into philanthropic activities, and actually work on making the world a better place, as he'd sometimes dreamed of as a kid when he'd been shunted from one foster home to the next.

Yeah, right. Patricia had pulled all his cockamamy dreams out from under him. The more fool he, he'd finally decided, after a month of moping, of letting his work flounder. True, he might get over her eventually— but what was the point of suffering such brutal heartache if a guy was just going to get over it and have a new woman kick him in the teeth? The smarter choice would be to find a sure bet, something that would pay off in the end. The IRA of women.

His dedicated assistant, Jane Fielding, fit the bill perfectly. Of course, his decision was colored by that single night, shortly after Patricia had bailed out on him, that

Jane had gone out for drinks with him, lent him a shoulder to cry on and, later, a bed in Brooklyn to sleep in....

He picked up the phone again and pressed redial. Still busy! What was she doing on the phone when they were supposed to be getting married?

Probably trying to locate him, he thought with irritation.

Bail out, a niggling little voice inside his head told him. Maybe this was an omen, a sign that he could never be happy with a fresh-faced kid from Vermont.

But alongside that cynical directive came another voice. A feminine voice. Jane's. *"I love you, Allan."*

The night they made love, she had said those words in the heat of passion. And every time he'd thought of them since, they stopped him in his tracks. *Loved him?*

He could count on the fingers of one hand the number of times he'd heard that phrase in his life. Certainly never from any of his foster parents. Never from his real ones, either, whom he could barely remember. But Jane—who had never so much as hinted that she was attracted to him before that night—had declared that she loved him.

Had she been telling the truth?

Some part of him, some vulnerable, foolish part of him, wanted to find out. To go ahead with the marriage. To accept that love and perhaps even return it. If he was even capable of such a thing anymore.

Was he?

Oh, sure. About as capable as a goat was of flying.

He stubbed out his cigarette and was preparing to turn the car back to New York City when a red ash flicked down onto the carpet at the foot of the passenger seat. Burn holes killed the resale value! Instinctively, he reached over to pat it out, using the floor mat as an extinguisher.

Certain the crisis had passed, he straightened up—and gasped. A huge black and white cow had stepped into the road, right in front of his path. Allan let out a string of curses and madly turned the steering wheel at the same time he hit the brakes.

An earsplitting squeal met his ears as those pristine treads grasped futilely at the slick pavement. His snazzy love car skidded crazily, avoiding the cow but still going too fast as it headed toward the ditch—and the telephone pole on the other side of it. As the Mercedes pitched over the rut, Allan clung to the steering wheel for dear life, not even letting go when his vehicle made direct contact with the telephone pole.

Something exploded, glass shattered, and the sickening sound of crunching metal ripped through the air. Then, just that quickly, all was silence, except for one mocking sound, the last noise Allan Steele would hear on what was supposed to be the day of his very practical wedding.

Moo.

Chapter One

The old grandfather clock in the corner of the flower-bedecked front parlor chimed another quarter hour, proclaiming, as if anyone needed to be reminded, that the groom was now a half hour late for his wedding. Jane glanced around at her loved ones, all trying their hardest to avoid looking her in the eye, and just barely kept herself from clutching her stomach as a wave of queasiness overcame her. Instead, she grasped her spring cascade bouquet in a death grip and tried to look confident.

She doubted anyone was fooled. She could feel the jilted-bride flush creeping up from her toes to the top of her head, and it didn't escape her notice that everyone winced when, warming up for her big ceremony solo, Aunt Katherine warbled out yet another verse of "Our Love Is Here to Stay," in the next room. They weren't wincing at Aunt Katherine's shaky soprano voice, either. Those winces were meant for Jane, acknowledging the fact that *her* love wasn't here at all. He wasn't even calling!

Jane looked over and saw her cousin on the phone again. Brenda, who had driven all the way over from Montpelier with Katherine, was calling home every five minutes to check on her baby-sitter. Jane felt her breath hitch—there was always that minuscule chance that Allan was trying to reach her—but then her shoulders sagged in resignation. It would just be too embarrassing to march across the room and remind Brenda that Allan might be attempting to call the house, when he certainly hadn't made the attempt after any of the other five times she'd told Brenda the very same thing.

Why, oh, why, had she ever agreed to have her wedding in Vermont, in front of all these people? Forever after, whenever she saw them, they would all remember this horrible day. Whenever she came home for a weekend or holidays, she would sit in this parlor...and feel shabby and humiliated all over again.

But of course she knew why she had agreed to the modest home ceremony. Her father. Will Fielding had wanted to do this for her. And since she had convinced *him* to retire, *he* was going to nag at her until she agreed to have a proper wedding.

It had only seemed fair. And her dad had thrown himself into the preparations. Even now, he couldn't help dragging people over to look at the cake—the hundred dollar cake, he called it. It was magnificent—three-tiered, done up with translucent sugared pansies, crowned with a plastic bridal couple who even looked suspiciously like Jane and Allan. Her father had prided himself on that detail especially. He had called her to find out what color Allan's hair was and found a groom that almost precisely matched Allan's brown hair and gray eyes.

But cake or no cake, she should have eloped. That was what Allan had wanted, and what she had wanted, too, in the beginning. She had known this was going to be a marriage based on practicality; she and Allan weren't even going to exchange rings. It was only her happiness—her incredible, unexpected giddiness—that had allowed her to be swayed by her father's wishes.

Well. Engaged as she was to "the barracuda of Wall Street," she should have anticipated a hitch. For years she had been Allan Steele's right hand as he made a killing on the market, had watched him with admiration as he ruthlessly made his millions, cannibalizing other firms and stealing their clients. Coming to Manhattan five years earlier with business school under her belt but a decided deficit in the department of big-business savvy, Jane had started working for Allan Steele and discovered a hero. To her, he seemed a miracle worker. A man whose very touch seemed to spin gold.

His tough, prickly persona and uninhibited ambition and drive were all characteristics that she had determined to cultivate in herself. Unfortunately, the seeds of ruthlessness just never took. Instead, she found her soft spot getting even softer—for Allan. Incredibly, she fell in love with the barracuda.

But he *wasn't* just a ruthless businessman, she had decided. Working with him day in and day out, she began to see in him what others didn't. What others called ruthlessness, she saw as a practicality that made his clients richer—precisely what a broker was supposed to do. And while some people called him workaholic, she thought of him merely as dedicated, focused.

Most important of all, where some saw heartlessness in Allan, she saw a heart tightly guarded. Witness his behavior after his breakup with Patricia Blakemore. Allan had been heartbroken, only most people—people who didn't understand him as well as Jane did—wouldn't have noticed. They didn't see that the little numbers he doodled on his desk blotter represented the amount he'd spent in the past fiscal year on flowers for Patricia and expensive dinner dates. Jane did.

And she was with him the night when his endearing brittleness seemed as if it would finally snap. They had both been working late one night, when suddenly Allan had asked her out for dinner. Not just for takeout, either. They went uptown for cocktails, then dinner, and then he escorted her back to her apartment in Brooklyn for a nightcap. And ended up staying the night. To Jane, it was like being Cinderella at the ball. For the first time in five years, Allan seemed to actually care about her as a person. That night, she had begun to believe that Allan could fall in love with her—eventually—an idea that gained credence when he asked her to marry him four weeks later.

But now, a mere three weeks after Allan's proposal, standing alone in her frilly wedding gown and watching old Reverend Woodwind surreptitiously check his watch, Jane knew without a doubt that she had been duped. Taken for a ride. Given the old snow job. How could she have allowed herself to fall for a man on the rebound? Allan, apparently, was going to walk away from their wedding day without another thought—and, in true barracuda fashion, without a pang of remorse. While she...

Well, she would probably get over the humiliation eventually. Someday she might even forget that Allan had dumped her so cold-bloodedly even after she had told him that she loved him. One thing she *couldn't* get over, or around, was the fact that she was going to have a baby. Allan's baby.

She hadn't wanted to tell him...hadn't had the nerve. It wasn't as if she had deliberately set out to entrap Allan, who had asked her to marry him a full week before that telltale pink stripe appeared on the home pregnancy test. She didn't see the point in telling him right away, in a rush. She wasn't even certain what tough-as-nails Allan would make of his impending fatherhood. Would he be angry? Indifferent? Overjoyed?

Was Allan ever overjoyed about anything?

Once they were married, she had decided, the news would probably be easier for him to digest. Frankly, she was afraid if she told him beforehand, he would bolt.

But now he had bolted anyway, and he had no excuse for doing so, as far as she could tell. Unless he had decided that he just didn't love her. Or *couldn't* love her.

That thought brought another wave of nausea crashing over her, and she was just looking toward the kitchen's swinging door, wondering whether anyone would notice if she sprinted through it, when suddenly her father was at her side.

"Jane, honey…" he said tentatively, in a near whisper.

Jane braced herself. She couldn't run now.

"I don't want to sound like some old doom-and-gloomer," her father continued, "but it sort of looks like…"

Poor man. Will Fielding was tall and lanky and had slightly stooped shoulders, thick iron-gray hair that he chopped into a buzz cut every two weeks at Charlie's in town, big ears and light blue eyes that right now resembled those of a particularly forlorn basset hound. His large, round eyes, with their endearingly droopy bags hanging below them, bore an expression of pure pain, and his forehead was a mass of worry wrinkles.

She took a deep breath and put a hand on her father's

arm to steady them both. "It doesn't just 'look like,' Dad. Face it, I've been stood up."

He made a low shushing noise. "You don't know that for sure, Janie."

Hearing his endearment of her name almost made her want to cry, or to throw herself into his arms as she had when she was nine and humiliated herself at her piano recital. She had blanked out right in the middle of "Old Dog Blue" in front of an audience of one hundred, and when she was finally able to crawl off that stage, she couldn't imagine anything worse happening to her.

Too bad she couldn't have had a crystal ball. Foreseeing this fiasco would have provided some cold comfort. Of course, it also might have provided the impetus she needed to hurl herself off the auditorium roof.

"Oh, Dad," she moaned. In the next room, she heard Aunt Katherine still singing on about love lasting longer than it would take for Gibraltar to crumble. "You can't think—"

He cut her off. "You know what I always say. Shouldn't ever make a judgment till all the facts are in. Sure, the man hasn't shown up. Doesn't mean he won't, though."

She used to be that optimistic, she remembered now. Back in the days before she moved to Manhattan, before she met Allan and tried to absorb his speculative, either snatch-your-profits or cut-your-losses methods. She'd spent years studying under the master of ruthless, thick-skinned practicality.

Today, apparently, she was going to receive her diploma.

Jane gestured to the hundred-dollar wedding cake. "Just look, Dad. The icing is beginning to sag. He's not coming."

Her father's brow sprouted a few more wrinkles.

"Reverend Woodwind's been looking at his watch for ten minutes now," she continued.

"Does he have another service to perform today?"

"No, he has a golf game with the bishop at noon."

Will Fielding shook his head. "I can't imagine what's happened."

"I got engaged to a barracuda, that's what."

"But what if there's been an accident?"

She rolled her eyes. *An accident!* That was what she had thought, too—for the first half hour. After that she realized she'd just been kidding herself.

This whole wedding was the result of her kidding herself. Oh, she'd known Allan didn't love her. She was no Patricia Blakemore. While Patricia, the love of Allan's life, was tall and statuesque, Jane herself was tall, but in a knobby, awkward kind of way. Patricia had perfectly dyed blond hair, bright blue eyes and perfect skin that was bronzed even in January. The woman could have been a poster child for Club Med. Jane, on the other hand, with her pale—she would say doughy—complexion, most closely resembled the legions of office workers whose only chance to see natural light came on the walk to and from the subway every day. But most important of all, Patricia had a sophisticated aggressive quality that Jane, for all her years on Wall Street, had never been able to cultivate.

But even against these odds, Jane had hoped that maybe, after a while, Allan might fall in love with her. If not exactly a picture-perfect set of lovebirds, she had imagined them being companions, partners. If nothing else, they would be proud parents of a little boy or girl.

Jane felt her anger rising. What a fool she'd been! Suddenly, her five years of idolizing Allan Steele just looked like five years wasted. Everyone had been right about him after all. The man had no heart. She had seen only what she wanted to see.

And now she would pay the consequences, and so would an innocent little child, who would grow up never knowing his or her father. At least, not if *she* had any say in the matter!

"Janie, are you all right?"

Her father's wrinkly eyes stared curiously into hers. "You went pale, and now you look feverish. Do you need to lie down?"

Lie down? What a question! That was the last thing she wanted to do. Because, suddenly, she realized that she wasn't going to take Allan's dumping her lying down. Nor was she going to crawl to him and try to wheedle him into a practical marriage for the baby's sake. The responsibility for her predicament, Jane realized, was all hers—well, almost all hers—and, by thunder, she would take care of herself.

For that matter, she wasn't going to allow Allan to jilt her. If anyone was going to any jilting, it was going to be *her!*

"I need to find Allan," she said.

Her father nodded. "Yes, dear, that *does* seem to be the problem."

She clarified her intention for him. "No, Dad, I need to find him so I can call off the wedding."

"*You're* calling off the wedding?" he asked, his eyebrows darting up almost to his scalp. He gave an up-and-down glance at her long, traditionally flouncy white wedding dress.

True, she wasn't dressed like someone wanting to duck out on a marriage. "This has been a mistake from the beginning," she said, turning to look at the phone.

Brenda still monopolized it, and was making kissy-kissy sounds long distance to her baby.

In the next room, Aunt Katherine hit a particularly tuneless note and held it. Jane winced as she strode over to the phone. "Do you mind?" she asked, hovering over cousin Brenda. "I need to make a call."

Her father was right on her heels. "Are you sure you aren't being too hasty?"

Jane felt a wave of guilt. She just couldn't admit to her father the full extent of the truth yet, couldn't explain that it was vitally important that she make a decision concerning Allan and stick to it.

She took the phone from Brenda and began dialing her number at work. The receptionist, Dawn, answered with a typically chirpy, "Steele and Grimly. How may I direct your call?"

Jane froze, speechless. Who would she ask for? Surely Allan wasn't mean enough to actually show up to work on what was supposed to be his wedding day. She didn't even want to ask. Dawn would recognize her voice, and though the marriage was supposed to be a secret from everyone except Allan's partner, Grady Grimly, word might have leaked out.... Of course, she could always talk to Grady, but that opened a whole different can of worms.

She dropped the handset back down on its cradle and turned, finding herself face-to-face with twenty wedding guests huddled around her.

"What happened?" her father asked.

"I, uh...couldn't remember the number." She knew it sounded lame, but it was the best she could do under pressure.

Luckily, at that moment the doorbell rang. Her father's face sagged with relief, but Jane stiffened, the courage that had failed her so miserably over the phone suddenly returning full force.

So! Allan had deigned—finally—to honor them with his presence!

"Thank goodness," her father breathed.

Aunt Katherine came galloping in with her sheet music. Obviously, the guests still expected a wedding, as did Reverend Woodwind, who was already beginning to thumb to the proper place in his prayer book.

Jane hated to disappoint them, but her decision not to marry Allan wasn't going to change just because her groom was shuffling in forty-five minutes late. If he was having second thoughts, that was fine. *She* wasn't going to be second-best, the best he could do, the next best thing. She wasn't going to embark on a marriage of convenience just because he was the father of her child, either.

Five years ago, she had transformed herself from farm girl to working girl. Now, she would have to change from working girl to single working mom. It might be a lot tougher, but she would have the satisfaction of not being anyone's mercy wife.

As she strode to the door the guests parted like the Red Sea before Moses, and Jane could feel her father practically on her heels.

"Now, Jane, don't say anything rash...."

"Not rash, Dad," she said. "I've been a good five years coming to this decision."

Five years. In those five years, she had seen co-workers who had started at Steele and Grimly the same time she did accumulate wealthy clients, hop to other investment houses, go on to fame and fortune. After five years, Jane was still working in the same cubicle attached to Allan's office, still his right hand. Her only clients were a few castoffs he had thrown her. And instead of fortune, the only thing she had collected was heartache.

It had taken her five years to come to her senses—and now she was coming to them with a vengeance.

The guests, sensing something very wrong, surged closer to the door, which Jane swept open with a proud, disdainful air, prepared to fling some harsh words at her erstwhile groom.

But instead of Allan, she found herself face-to-face with a policeman. A policeman wearing a very grave expression.

"ALLAN, CAN YOU HEAR me?"

Of course he couldn't. He was unconscious. Still, as Jane looked at his nicked and bruised face, and the huge bandage swathing his head where it had hit the windshield of his car, she couldn't help trying to speak to him, to reach out to him.

"Allan, please, you've *got* to wake up."

Those last words seemed to have an effect on him—she could have sworn she noticed his eyelids twitch. For a moment she held her breath, hoping to catch another glimpse of movement, but he was still again, except for his breathing.

She walked around to the foot of the bed. It was almost six o'clock in the evening, a full six hours after the policeman had announced that there had been an automobile accident not far from their house, involving a Mercedes convertible. Jane had been so distressed, she would have jumped in the police car in her wedding dress if her father hadn't told her it would probably be better if she took off her gown before going to the hospital. Even so, she had thrown on the first thing she'd laid eyes on—the plain off-white linen dress that she had meant to be her going-away outfit, although their honeymoon was only going to be a working weekend in his Upper East Side penthouse.

Honeymoon. She looked at Allan and couldn't help feeling a pang of regret. Even with all his bandages and bruises, he was so handsome. She felt herself moving, drawn as if by a powerful force, back to his side again. *If only things were different...*

"Oh, Allan," she said with a sigh, combing a lock of hair away from his brow with her hand, "why do you have to be a barracuda? Why couldn't you be nice?" She felt moisture pooling in her eyes and leaned away from him again.

His eyes twitched again, especially hard this time, and no wonder. *Nice* was just not a word that suited Allan Steele, and apparently it never would.

She had to admit, when the policeman had told her about the accident, her heart had filled with hope. Hope that Allan was all right, and hope that this was the reason he had been late for the wedding. But one disturbing fact was impossible to put out of her mind. When the Mercedes was discovered, it was pointed west—*away* from Jane's father's farm. The map she herself had drawn up had been right there in the crumpled front seat, so there seemed no way Allan could have missed the fact that he had just passed up the farm's entrance gate.

Unless he'd done so on purpose.

Unless he'd changed his mind about the whole wedding.

Anger began to rise in her again, and she stepped back again from the hospital bed. It was wrong to feel like throttling a man who had just had a close encounter

g. But this...this *comment* coming from Allan
ally unexpected. And not just because he hadn't
ized her.

se. It almost seemed as if he—Allan Steele, the
uda himself—expected her to *flirt* with him!
better get the doctor,'' she said anxiously, and
for the door.

ESIA?''

McGillicutty was unruffled as they came out of
s room. ''A little memory loss isn't too out of the
ry in head trauma cases such as this,'' he said.
ut he doesn't seem to remember *anything*,'' she
im.

shrugged. ''Given a little time...''

sentence trailed off, frustrating Jane with its very
niteness. She could hardly tell Allan that the wed-
was off when he couldn't even remember it. Yet
uldn't really go about her business as usual with
atter unsettled, especially with a little bundle of
the way. How long would she have to remain in
emarital limbo?

ow much time?'' she asked the doctor.

e a true medical professional, he evaded her ques-
'What that man needs is peace and quiet and lots
.''

llan's not going to like that,'' Jane replied, men-
witching hats as she started thinking like Allan's
hand again. ''Of course, if we set him up in his
hent...''

doctor looked concerned. ''In New York?''

f course. That's where Allan lives.''

shook his head. ''It would be better for Mr. Steele

with a telephone pole—she knew that. But the fact that
he had been going to just drive away, leaving her to
face all their guests alone, without giving her so much
as an explanation...well, she *did* feel like shaking the
man silly. She looked down at her ever-so-slightly
thickened middle and realized that she would be throttling for two now.

While it was true that Allan didn't have any idea that
she was going to have a baby, shouldn't he have at least
considered the possibility? If memory served her correctly, she hadn't been alone in her apartment when the
baby was conceived. Although she'd been more alone
than she realized, apparently.

Well, fine. She didn't need him. Everything from
middle-of-the-night feedings to scraping up college tu-
ition might be harder without a husband by her side,
but she wouldn't be the first single mother in the world.
Allan would never even need to know the baby was his.

In fact, the minute she knew he was able to hear her,
she was going to tell him that their relationship—aside
from their professional one—was over. She wished she
didn't have to work at Steele and Grimly anymore, but
with a baby on the way, quitting wouldn't be the practical thing to do at this juncture. Hopefully, she would
be able to find a new job soon. Until then, as long as
they did have to spend day after day in each other's
company, she wanted to make it clear to him that *she*
had decided that they were through.

Her naturally pragmatic mind had already turned to
the thorny issue of switching health insurance policies
in mid-pregnancy, when Allan's eyelids fluttered.

''Allan?'' Temporarily forgetting her anger, she
dashed to his side, leaning so close she was practically

climbing over the steel safety rail. "Allan, can you hear me?"

She received no response.

Dr. McGillicutty had assured her that Allan would make a complete recovery. The air bag had softened his head's collision with the window, and besides a sprained arm, his injuries were mostly superficial. Chances were, the doctor had said with a chuckle, Allan would be back to his old self in no time at all, and they could go ahead with their wedding.

"We're not going to be married," Jane had informed the doctor right there in the middle of the hallway, amid the bustling nurses and patients on gurneys momentarily stalled.

The doctor's reassuring expression became an anxious frown. "But, on the hospital admittance form, you wrote that you were his fiancée. Your father said—"

Jane nodded. "I am—I mean I was."

"Then Mr. Steele called off the wedding?"

She tried not to take offense. "Actually," she corrected, "no one's called it off yet. But I intend to, just as soon as I can."

"Oh, my," the doctor said. "Of course, it's none of my—"

"If you're worried about my right to be here, I *am* Mr. Steele's assistant," she had assured the man. "To Allan's way of thinking, that's an even more important relationship than next of kin."

Unfortunately, she was afraid those flippant words were the truth. Looking at Allan now, helpless in the hospital bed, with one of the strong arms that had once held her close now imprisoned in a sterile-looking sling, she could almost manage to feel pity for him. He had no one, and might never have anyone. Patricia had for-

saken him, and now his second stab crumpled as completely as the front des.

Allan's eyelids flickered again, the It took a moment for the pupils of his to the fluorescent lighting in the clini to swallow past the dryness in his m I?"

Against her will, Jane's heart pick dear, raspy, cigarette-ravaged voice a pital in Vermont."

His eyes widened in surprise. "Ver ter a moment of thought, he asked, "

"A nurse?" Jane blinked in conf know her? "No."

He closed his eyes again. "I tho dress."

She looked down at what was suppo her alluring trousseau outfit and fe Maybe it *did* look a little like a nurse' never had very flashy taste.

"I'm Jane," she reminded him, f turbed her that he couldn't remember v ter all, they had been minutes away fro when he'd run into that pole! And eve fiancée didn't ring a bell, there were th dedicated service....

"Just Jane?"

She pursed her lips wryly. "Just pla

His gray eyes opened again, and a un-Allan-like grin spread across his lip

Jane opened her mouth to speak, b her she couldn't figure out how to rep stered herself to tell Allan that she was if he stayed here. Traveling wouldn't improve his condition.''

"Here?"

The doctor sent her a speculative look. "Didn't your father say he owned a dairy farm nearby?''

Much as she hated the idea of Allan staying for heaven only knew how long in an impersonal hospital room, the idea of him staying on her father's farm seemed even worse. "You want Allan to stay *there?*''

"Relaxation is what that man needs,'' the doctor said. "No work.''

"But Allan works to relax,'' Jane said.

McGillicutty shook his head. "Well...not so much work then. And what your fiancé needs—''

"He's not my fiancé,'' Jane reminded him.

"Your *boss* then,'' the man corrected. "What he needs is quiet. Clean air.''

She looked at him skeptically. "Allan *hates* quiet, and clean air makes him sick.''

The unshakable doctor was beginning to look unnerved. "Look, Miss Fielding, if you want Mr. Steele to recover, I'm afraid you'll have to follow my advice.''

Of course she wanted him to recover. For one thing, she could hardly wait to give him a piece of her mind!

If the doctor said peace and quiet, how could she refuse?

"Oh, all right,'' she agreed. "I'll tell my father.''

"That's good,'' the doctor said. "Mr. Steele should be discharged tomorrow morning. We're only keeping him tonight to monitor his concussion.''

Jane frowned, feeling as if she'd just been granted custody of a small child. She couldn't leave Allan alone in Vermont—which meant that she would have to play nursemaid to him. Which also meant she would have to be in constant contact with him, looking into those sexy gray eyes that would be persistent reminders of the fact that she had been oh-so-close to becoming Mrs. Allan Steele.

Before she had wised up.

"How long?" she asked again.

"What?" the doctor asked, his eyebrows raised.

"How long until Allan recovers his memory?"

Dr. McGillicutty hesitated. "It could be hours...but then, it could be a matter of months."

Jane bit back a sigh of frustration at the man's elliptic predictions.

"Oh, and Miss Fielding," the doctor continued, "it would be best if Mr. Steele were kept from having any kind of emotional shock."

She blinked in confusion. "What do you mean?"

The doctor folded his arms. "Maybe you had better not broach the subject of the wedding for a while. I can understand your wanting to sort out your marital situation, but perhaps in this case later would be better than sooner."

If she couldn't mention the wedding, how was she going to get Allan's memory back so she could tell him what a rat he was?

"Just keep him comfortable," the doctor said, patting Jane on the shoulder before bustling down the hall to his next patient.

Jane bit her lip and considered. *Comfortable.* She knew just how to keep the barracuda comfortable.

Chapter Two

He woke to the feel of sun pouring through the window, a ravenous rumbling in his stomach and a pounding in his head that must have followed him home that morning from the hospital.

Home.

Allan opened one eye to inspect his surroundings. This wasn't his home, of course—he was nearly certain that nowhere he had lived had ever looked like this. The old double bed was adorned with acorn knobs on the posters. The walls around him were pale yellow with bright white trim; on one hung an oil landscape. On an old maple bureau, the top of which was covered with a lace doily, strangers smiled in wood and silver frames. Flower-sprigged patterned curtains dangled from the windows. And from the picture window across the room a breeze blew gently toward Allan.

Clean, fresh air. He sighed happily, then closed his eyes again. A bird twittered insistently outside. Was that what had opened his eyes—or had it been the odd feeling of awakening in a strange, antique bed with a soft springy mattress and a warm snuggly quilt? Or had it been the unusually sweet dream he'd been having of Jane, his beautiful nurse?

He smiled. *Employee,* she had informed him sternly when he had asked her their relationship in the hospital. She had told him little else—except that he "wasn't himself." The doctor, putting it more bluntly, told him he had amnesia.

Well, whoever he was, he sure had good taste in employees.

His mouth opened in a big yawn, then he felt his lips curling into a happy grin. The headache didn't matter. His sprained arm didn't matter. He was in Jane's house, in a comfy bed, with nothing to do all day but daydream. And mostly, he knew, his daydreams would probably center on the beautiful woman who had hovered around him all night at the hospital, until she had apologetically informed him that morning that he was being taken to her father's farm to recuperate—as if he would object!

What kind of fool wouldn't love to be laid up with a pretty woman on a picture-perfect old farm in Vermont?

As he looked out the window, he let out another long sigh, which slowly transformed into a hum. Which in turn led him to singing a bar of an old Beatles tune. The chorus of "Good Day, Sunshine" was all he could remember, so he repeated it with more gusto, adding a little drumroll with the his right hand, which was the only one he had free at the moment, since his left was stiffly wrapped and encased in a sling.

His gaze was distracted—and his hand halted in mid-drum—by Jane poking her head through the door. Her eyebrows knit together and her mouth turned down in a quizzical frown. "Allan?"

"Good day, sunshine," he singsonged, willing to be

any kind of silly if it would wipe that worried look off her face.

Her frown deepened, and Jane lingered half in and half out of the room. "Are you feeling all right?"

"Never better. Come on in," he said.

A tentative smile touched her lips. "I've brought you a surprise."

"Breakfast?" Allan asked. His stomach rumbled hungrily. A tray of bacon, eggs and hot buttered toast would be perfect.

"Better." She had something hidden behind her back as she approached the bed—something too small for a breakfast tray, he noted with disappointment.

Nevertheless, he loved a surprise, and even more important, he was glad of Jane's company. She was dressed more casually today, though even in jeans and an old flannel work shirt, she somehow managed to look all business. Perhaps it was the way her short brown hair was bobbed in such an orderly fashion. Or the normally unassuming look in her green eyes, which now held a hint of anticipation as she gazed down at him.

"I can't guess what it could be," he said.

"Ta-dah!" With a flourish, she produced a small gray plastic case. "It survived. Can you believe it?"

He gazed at the object, a computer notebook, then looked back into Jane's eyes. "Oh."

"Isn't that wonderful?" She folded her arms over her chest. "Well, it was practically a miracle, considering that your Mercedes is beyond repair."

Although he had been told about his car being totaled before, hearing the news again caused a tremor to go through him—almost as if he had lost his best friend. But that couldn't be. Probably he was instinctively reacting to his narrow escape from death.

But as for the notebook... "I guess I forgot about it," he said, trying to work up some excitement for the thing.

"I knew you would have brought it with you," she explained. "It was found in the back seat. I even have the cord, and an extension, so you'll be able to work in bed. Isn't that great?"

Great. Wonderful. Did she really expect him to *work?*

"The doctor told me I shouldn't bother myself with work, remember?"

She dismissed this medical advice with a shrug and a wave. "Well, of course, a doctor *would* say that. But for you, it would be more like playing."

She dropped to her hands and knees and started rooting around beside the headboard. "What are you doing?" he asked, leaning over the side of the bed.

"Plugging you in." She was bent down on all fours, her head somewhere under or behind the bed, her knobby elbows jutting out to her sides, her shapely backside pointing up.

"You don't have to do that...."

"It's no trouble," she said, moments before he heard the sound of a thud. "Ouch!"

Startled, he pushed himself closer and laid his hand over her shoulder. Her whole body tensed, and she banged her head against the bedside table again. "Ouch!"

"Be careful," he told her, laughing gently, "or you'll wind up with a headache like mine."

She turned and looked at him with sincere concern in her green eyes. "Your head hurts?"

"Just a little."

"No wonder you didn't light up at the sight of your notebook! Why didn't you tell me?"

"It's nothing, really," he began, but her head disappeared under the bed again.

"Got it!" she cried triumphantly. She suddenly straightened and set up the laptop on the quilt in front of him. When he merely stared at the thing, she flipped a switch. Instantly the little machine came to life, humming and beeping cheerily.

Jane beamed at him. "I'll bet you're glad to see your old friend again."

Considering this whirring machine was the first friend of his she had mentioned in two days, Allan began to get a little nervous. He grinned limply. "Sure am."

She sent him a puzzled look, then suddenly frowned. "Your headache!" she cried apologetically. "I'm so sorry, I'll get the medication the doctor sent home with us. That will get rid of the pain, and then you'll be able to work, work, work to your heart's content."

Where was all this talk about work coming from?

He managed to capture her arm before she could speed off. "Wait. It's not that serious. Just morning grogginess, mostly."

Her eyes widened in dismay. "How could I forget? You're probably going through caffeine withdrawal! I'll be right back." She tugged free and did a three-yard dash toward the door. "Don't worry, Allan," she tossed over her shoulder, "we'll have you back to your old self in no time!"

Allan flopped back against the pillows and discovered that his head truly was beginning to throb now. Jane was so jumpy! Why? And why was she so eager to get him back to his "old self"?

Allan didn't even know who that person was. He looked at the menu on the screen of his computer. Filling the page were lists of names. He supposed now was as good a time as any to start investigating himself. At least he could figure out what he did for a living. He scanned the files and clicked his mouse on SIMIN.ACC.

Immediately, the screen filled with an eye-popping display of numbers. Allan moaned. Just staring at the screen made his headache worse. Quickly, he punched the escape key and put the notebook computer aside.

Within seconds, Jane was back with the hoped-for tray. But when she laid it in front of him, he and his grumbling stomach noted that there was no food. Just a cup of coffee, a pill and a stack of newspapers.

"This morning I went to town and picked up copies of *The New York Times, The Wall Street Journal, The Washington Post*—oh, and look underneath—it's the newest issue of *Forbes.* I *knew* you'd be excited about that!"

"Wow..." Allan said. "You've been a busy beaver this morning." But did she really expect him to read all this? Allan put the *Post,* the only one with comics in it, on the top of the pile. He would read them after Jane left.

All he was really in the mood for right now was conversation. "The coffee smells good," he said.

"I made it just how you like it. It'll probably be a relief after that watered-down hospital stuff."

He smiled as he lifted the cup to his lips. Whatever he paid Jane, it couldn't be enough. It probably didn't matter whether he had a memory or not—Jane knew him better than he knew himself. If he didn't remember something, he could be sure she would. He took a sip of the rich black brew, swallowed it happily—and then nearly slammed the red-and-white-patterned china cup back onto its matching saucer in horrified response.

The inky liquid was so strong, so bitter and so sick-

eningly sweet that it was barely recognizable as coffee.
His poor taste buds screamed in agony. It took everything in his power not to break into shuddering contor-
tions as the liquid burned its way down to his stomach.

"Just the way you like it," Jane said in a satisfied
chirp. "Triple-triple."

Allan winced. "T-triple?" His tongue was experi-
encing convulsions.

"Triple strength with three tablespoons of sugar. You
say it's invigorating."

That much was true. Every cell in his body was wide-
awake. In agony, but awake.

Jane smiled brightly. "Well. Now that you're in the
land of the living, I can give you the good news."

That sounded hopeful. "What?"

"The Dow's up forty-three points."

He blinked. "The what?"

She frowned. "The Dow Jones Industrial Average,
Allan."

"Oh, yes, of course." He hesitated a moment, not
certain to what heights of elation this information was
supposed to send him. "Up's better than down, I
guess," he said finally, forcing a smile.

She looked so distressed by his reaction that he nearly
felt guilty about not doing handsprings. "I really am
glad," he assured her.

"No, you're not." Shoulders sagging slightly, she sat
down at the foot of the bed. "None of this rings a bell,
does it?" she asked, gesturing to the papers, the computer, the coffee cup.

Allan shook his head slowly, regretfully. She had
tried so hard to duplicate his old morning routine, and
now she was crestfallen. But why was she so upset that
he hadn't popped immediately back to his old self?

Given what he knew of his old self so far—a friendless, caffeine addicted workaholic—it didn't sound like there was much to miss. Several times in the hospital he had asked her to tell him all about himself, but she'd shied away from anything except the barest facts.

Maybe, he thought, if he asked Jane something about herself, she might become more comfortable talking to him about personal matters. "So...why don't you tell me about you?"

"Me?" she asked, looking at him suspiciously. "What's there to tell?"

"I don't know," he said with a chuckle. "That's why I asked."

She sent him a wary glance. "I'm twenty-seven. I grew up here. I live in Brooklyn." She shrugged. "That's about it, I guess."

"I met your father," he said, coaching her. "Does your mother live here, too?"

She frowned. "No, my mother died of cancer when I was twelve."

"Oh." Something about that pricked at the edge of his memory. He had known a loss like that, he was certain. His own parents? "I'm sorry."

She shook her head. "My father is wonderful. I guess I'm glad to have the chance for a prolonged visit."

"Then my accident was fortuitous."

A stricken expression crossed her face.

He still wasn't sure what the circumstances were that had led him to Vermont, but judging from Jane's expression, it couldn't have been anything pleasant.

"There has to be something more you can tell me about yourself. Are you seeing someone?" he asked, trying to turn to a lighter topic.

"Seeing?" She appeared almost wounded by the question.

He laughed anxiously. "I wouldn't like to think that my recuperation was standing in the way of true romance."

Her lips twisted in a scowl. "No, of course it's not."

Allan grinned. Poor Jane definitely needed someone to show her how to lighten up. "Why 'of course'? Have you taken a vow of celibacy?"

"No…" She shifted uncomfortably, and he noticed one of her hands had taken hold of a fold of the quilt and was in the process of wringing the stuffing out of it.

There was something she wasn't telling him, and he wasn't going to give her peace until she let him know what it was.

"Since you don't want to talk about yourself, why not try telling more about me?"

"I've already told you some.…"

He frowned. "There must be more to know than my birth date and where I went to college. Who are my friends?" He patted his PC. "Besides Mr. IBM here?"

She shrugged. "I don't know."

Now it was his turn to be astonished. "You can't name *one?*"

"Well, there's Grady Grimly, your business partner. You two went to Harvard Business School together."

He smiled, relieved to know there was at least one person out there who liked him.

"But you haven't been getting along lately."

"Oh." So much for that one person. "Well…what do I do in my spare time?"

"You don't have any spare time."

He laughed. "That's crazy! No one works all the time."

"You do," she informed him soberly.

He frowned. The more he heard about himself, the more he was beginning to wish he were someone else. "Is there anything *good* you can tell me?"

Jane sat before him for an endless thirty seconds, her face tense with concentration. Finally she offered optimistically, "You exercise at your club every morning at eleven o'clock, and you adhere to a high-fiber, low-fat diet. You're in fantastic shape."

Which, from the sound of it, meant that he had a long tedious life of nonstop work ahead of him. Still, health was something.

"Except, of course," Jane added, "for the fact that you smoke two packs of cigarettes per day."

Wonderful.

She stood. "Which reminds me, I bought a pack at the store this morning. They're not your usual brand, but I know you like to have your morning puff with your coffee and paper."

She handed him the cellophane-wrapped package, which he took. She watched him eagerly as he examined the wrapper. "Aren't you going to have one?" she asked.

Something about the cigarettes seemed less than appetizing to him. "I don't think I should," he said, then pointed to the Surgeon General's warning. "Look. These things are bad for you."

"Well, yes..." Jane looked uncomfortable in the role of drug pusher. "But don't you think you'd feel more like your old self puffing on one?"

"That's what I'm afraid of," he said wryly.

"But you must want to get your memory back!"

"As long as I'm not craving one, it can be our little experiment to see how long I go before I start twitching in withdrawal."

"Would you like some more coffee, then?" she asked.

He looked down in dismay at the thick black liquid. "I think I'll be able to break that habit, too."

She crossed her arms again, then stood, resigned. "Well. Dad had some stuff he wanted to do, and I'm sure you'll want to get to work." She sent him a long, questioning stare. "Right?"

"Wrong."

Her frown deepened, and she tossed up her hands. "I knew this was a bad idea. You're probably dying to get back to the city, back to your apartment." Again there was a pause, almost as if she hoped he would agree with her. "Right?"

"Wrong again," he said with a smile as he stretched contentedly. "I think I could stay in Vermont forever." Curious to see how she would react, he threw caution to the wind and sent her a wink, adding, "As long as you're here, that is."

His remark was rewarded with a blush and two mortified green eyes. She began to edge toward the door. "I—I'm going to call the doctor about the pain medication he put you on," she said, "then I'll check on you later." She dashed out the door.

By the way she said later, he assumed she meant *much* later.

Maybe Jane wasn't accustomed to being winked at, he noted. She was even more uncomfortable with being flirted with than she was being asked about herself.

He shook his head. She had a secret. The question

was, how long would it be before he was able to get it out of her?

JANE HELD UP a pair of leather running shoes and felt herself grinning like a fool. For the past two days, it seemed all she had done was dangle objects in front of Allan in hopes that one of them would finally ring a bell of recognition inside his head. But so far, all she'd received for her efforts were stares as blank as the one he was sending her now.

"Isn't this a rather literal way to try to jog my memory?" he joked.

Joked! Apparently, all her efforts to restore Allan to his old taciturn self were fruitless.

She frowned. "It was Monday and the stores were open, so I decided to go into town to see if they had any shoes in your size. You only have your nice clothes here, and since you're accustomed to physical activity…"

He didn't look overly enthusiastic. Nevertheless, he reached out for the shoes. "Thanks. I don't know the last time a woman bought me sneakers."

"Last year." He raised his brows and she clarified. "You sent me out to get a pair."

He nodded, and kept staring at her. As usual, the more he looked, the more awkward she felt. He had an overblown, appreciative way of gazing at her with those gray eyes of his that made her squirm. It was so thorough, so filled with speculation…so *un*-Allan-like.

It was tempting to give up on the old Allan in hopes that he would never return again. Then she wouldn't have to worry about her hurt pride, or getting even, or perhaps even her impending single motherhood. She could imagine telling this new flirtatious incarnation of her old boss that they had been on the verge of getting married, and having him go on with the ceremony as previously planned. She felt a smile tug at her lips just at the thought. How long would she be able to get away with it?

But of course she wouldn't do that. Couldn't. Taking up with the new Allan would be like renting a room in a fool's paradise. Someday, Allan would remember that he had been fleeing from her before the accident, and he would resent her all the more if she had trapped him into marriage...and into fatherhood.

No, it was the old Allan she had unfinished business with. It was the old Allan she needed to restore—no matter how stubbornly persistent this new incarnation was.

She heard Allan's deep chuckle, felt his baritone rumble through her right down to her toes. "I don't believe I've ever met anyone like you," he said, shaking his head.

"That's because you have a bad memory," she answered. "I'm sure I'm not the only person like myself out there."

"Not too bad a memory," he corrected. "At least, I've discovered that a mere word can set me to remembering again."

Jane swallowed. "Like...what?"

He frowned, concentrating. "The word *barracuda* seems to ring a bell. Do you know anyone called by that unflattering name?"

She felt her heart skip a beat. Thank heavens! This was the first thing Allan had remembered of his old self. Maybe this was a beginning.... "You never considered it an insult, Allan."

His face paled and his eyes widened. "You mean *I'm* the barracuda?"

"Yes!" she said, coming forward. "But if you don't start getting back to your old self, they're liable to start calling you the minnow." She dared to move closer. "Don't you remember anything else about your old life?"

"Like what?"

"Well...what about your partner, Grady Grimly? Surely you remember him."

"You said I was having problems with him. Are we good friends?"

Jane frowned. "I doubt Grady's had a close relationship in his life, except with his psychiatrist. The man was born with the proverbial silver spoon in his mouth—a whole set of flatware, really—yet he still lives in panic that he's on the brink of ruin. Now he's decided that marriage will calm him down."

Jane hesitated to use the word *marriage* in front of Allan. She wanted him to get his memory back, but she still remembered Dr. McGillicutty's warning about no emotional shocks.

But apparently the word hadn't been significant enough to Allan to ring any bells. "Grady sounds like a strange one, all right," he said.

She paused a moment, then said, "He thinks marriage to *me* is just the answer."

That got Allan's attention. "Really?" He was at her side immediately. "Has he asked you to marry him?"

"Many times."

She couldn't help but be flattered by Allan's reaction to this news. The old Allan, her own fiancé, hadn't batted an eyelash, hadn't even seemed the slightest bit disturbed, when she informed him that his partner had been proposing to her for months. If anything, he seemed a little relieved to finally understand why Grady had been so unfriendly toward him lately. But the new Allan looked positively put out.

"I suppose I shouldn't bad-mouth a person when I don't even know him." At her dubious glance, he winced slightly. "Don't *remember* knowing him," he corrected.

"There's no reason—"

"But you're not going to marry a guy like this Grady character, are you?"

Jane folded her arms. Should she tell him that she had actually been prepared to go one worse and marry *him?* Only the memory of Dr. McGillicutty's severe expression stopped her. "What's the matter with him?"

Allan began pacing in agitation. "You just got finished telling me that he has no friends besides his psychiatrist—that hardly speaks well of him."

Jane cocked her head. "Well...everyone has their little quirks."

"Quirks!" Allan said, tossing up his hands. "The man sounds like a sociopath."

She had to laugh at that. "Believe me, there's nothing evil about Grady. He's perfectly harmless."

Allan harrumphed.

Jane lifted her shoulders. "Well, I suppose I'd better get back to work."

"You're working here?" Allan asked, concerned.

"Just a little research into the Clyde Simington file." At Allan's blank look, she reminded him, "Clyde's a client you're very interested in acquiring. We were working on his portfolio when—"

Jane froze. *When you asked me out for dinner...the time we spent the night together.* Her face felt as if it were about to go up in flames; she hoped Allan didn't pick up on it.

"You like this Simington fellow?" Allan asked.

"Of course. He's a real sweetheart."

Allan scowled.

"Allan?" She stepped closer to him, concerned.

He reached out to take her hand, sending a sensual shiver right down to the marrow of her bones. "Please, as your boss, I'm begging you to take the afternoon off. And as a man, I'm hoping you'll stop thinking about this Clyde Simington as well."

Did he think she was attracted to Clyde? "It's not—"

Suddenly, Allan tugged her hand and brought her closer to him. Before she could so much as take a breath, he leaned down and pressed his warm lips against hers. Every atom in Jane's body came instantly alive, and her arms moved of their own accord to snake their way behind Allan's neck.

He might be different personality-wise, but his kiss was enticingly familiar, bringing to mind the only time before that he had kissed her, which also was the time when he had made love to her. His good arm pressed gently against her back, bringing her ever closer to him. Though his sling was an awkward barrier between them, she could feel the heat radiating from his chest, felt her stomach do a flip-flop in response.

Shamelessly, she strained toward him without a thought in her head besides wonder at how much she wanted this man, and perhaps always would. It wasn't because he was the father of the child growing inside her that she reveled in the warmth she felt as his tongue pushed its way past her lips, where it began a subtle mating dance with her own tongue. It was simply because she seemed to have found the one man on earth she had a weakness for.

But now he was acting as if he had a weakness for her, too. The other time, he'd kissed her quickly, passionately. But now, she had the feeling that he was enjoying taking his time with her, romancing her there in the guest room of her father's house, seducing her with a slow, sensual kiss.

Maybe this would jar his memory, she thought vaguely as his light touch at her lower back sent a shiver of pleasure through her. It was certainly ringing bells in her head! All her running after him with papers and computers and shoes seemed pointless now, and nowhere near as pleasant. Maybe this would remind Allan Steele who he was, and what they had been to each other....

She sucked in her breath. "Oh, no!" she cried, pushing back from his chest. She was supposed to be gearing up to tell Allan off, not swooning in his arms! Where was her backbone? All she was doing was setting herself up for another fall.

He blinked in confusion. "Oh, no, what?"

"Never mind," she said, backing away.

He looked completely perplexed. "Jane, wait—"

"No, I'll see you at dinner."

She dashed out the door and thundered down the stairs to the kitchen, where her father sat at a table, snacking.

"Heavens to Betsy!" Will cried. "What's happened to you?"

"What makes you ask?" she replied, straightening her hair with her hand.

He turned those blue eyes on her, then laughed. "You might do a fair job at playing Florence Nightingale, sweetheart, but Meryl Streep you're not. Looks to me like you're blushing."

"I am not," she said, but she could feel the temperature rising in her cheeks even as she voiced the denial. She looked at the plate her dad was munching and moaned. On it was a piece of the hundred-dollar cake. "Oh, Dad—you've got to stop eating that cake. If Allan saw you—"

"I paid good money for this cake. 'Course I'm gonna eat it."

"Well at least don't let Allan see it. At lunch you put some on his tray, and I noticed him eyeing it suspiciously. If he did manage to piece together—"

Will threw up his hands. "I don't get it. Three days ago you were supposed to be married, then Allan apparently changed his mind, so you changed your mind, but then it turned out you've got a groom who can't even remember anything about you. And now we're supposed to tippy-toe around so that while he's gettin' his memory back, he *won't* remember the wedding."

"So what's wrong with that?" Jane asked.

"It doesn't make sense. Why don't you just do as planned and marry the man, and worry about his memory later?"

She rolled her eyes. "I've explained this, Dad. You just don't know Allan."

Her father shrugged. "The man doesn't seem so much like a piranha to me, hon."

"Barracuda," Jane corrected absently, her mind still on the feel of Allan's lips against hers. "*This* man's not a barracuda."

"Then why don't you marry him?"

"Because this isn't the man I was engaged to," Jane explained in exasperation.

"But you said the old Allan was meaner."

"He was."

"Then wouldn't that make this one the better choice for a husband?"

"Of course," she answered, shaking her head. "But the old Allan is bound to return, and then I'm going to be stuck with him. So it's better to get rid of the new Allan, so I can get rid of the old Allan, too. Then I can start fresh." She took a breath. "You see?"

Her father scratched his head. "All I can see is that this one seems to be crazy for you."

Jane took a breath. *Was* this Allan crazy for her—or was that just some aberration created by that bump on the noggin he'd taken? There was plenty of evidence to back up her father's assertion. Aside from their kiss, he seemed always to be touching her—putting his hand over hers, or on her shoulder. She still had a bump on her head the size of a lemon from his gentle pat when she'd been trying to plug in the computer. Then there were those smiles of his—long, lazy grins that made her quiver in response. Who could have guessed that Allan Steele had such a devastatingly sexy smile?

The answer was simple. *She* could have. But only in her wildest dreams had she ever imagined all that suppressed sexiness being aimed at *her*. Even after they had slept together, the old Allan had been his same driven self around her. He certainly hadn't winked at her—wouldn't have given her the afternoon off and then pulled her to him like a modern-day Valentino!

"I like him," her father said.

"He stood me up at my wedding!" she cried, the memory still stinging.

"But he didn't. He had an accident."

"He was trying to sneak away, Dad. His car wasn't even headed toward our gate."

"Maybe that's not what it seemed, honey."

"Oh, Dad—you never want to believe the worst of people," she said. "But I've got to be realistic." *I've got a child to consider....* She wished she could tell her father, but she wasn't certain how he was going to take this news. Sure, there was no one nicer than Will Fielding, but he did have that old-fashioned streak.

He would probably *insist* that she get married!

"Besides," she said, "when you think about it, you don't really know *either* Allan very well."

He looked out the window, nodding toward Allan, who was strolling through the back pasture. He had on the sneakers Jane had given him, which were glaringly white in contrast with his gray suit pants. The shoes had obviously put a lively spring in his step. He practically skipped through the grass, never minding how goofy he might appear, and bent down occasionally to pick a wildflower and add it to the collection in the hand peeping out of his cast.

"Sometimes you *can* judge a man just by looking at him," her father said. "Your Allan has a kind face."

"He's not *my* Allan," Jane corrected quickly, but then she looked at him, his smile, the bright expression in his face, and felt herself melt a little. Her head knew she wanted nothing to do with Allan Steele, but her heart was harder to persuade.

Chapter Three

God, he loved Vermont! Loved the fresh, sweet-smelling air, the green, green landscape and the sense of peace and relaxation he felt here. He loved being around Jane…loved kissing her.

Allan bent down and picked another flower with his good arm. Something in the action felt very unfamiliar—and not just because of the awkwardness caused by his other arm in its sling. No, he had a tiny flash—a vague memory that seemed to tease him with increasing frequency—a sense that he was the type who didn't ordinarily pick flowers.

Who was he? Given Jane's grim hints these past few days, he figured he was probably the type of man who ordered flowers—ordered someone else to order them, that is. Probably Jane.

There was something about that woman that made him not worry about who he had been—just who he was going to be from now on. He felt a niggling emptiness inside himself, and instinctively wanted to turn to Jane to patch it up. Maybe that was wrong. Maybe she looked on him as simply her boss, or more likely, a nuisance.

Maybe he could change her mind.

He indulged himself for a moment, remembering their brief but very intimate kiss. He probably shouldn't have done it, but somehow, he just couldn't imagine her walking out the door without knowing what it would feel like to have her in his arms, to taste her delectably soft lips.

He smiled and looked down at his bouquet. Why did he have the feeling that Jane wouldn't appreciate his flower-picking efforts on her behalf any more than she had appreciated his kissing her? She was so guarded! He could understand if she was uncomfortable with him flirting with her at the office. But here? Out in the middle of the beautiful country, how could anyone think of anything else but romance?

She was a puzzle, but one he was determined to piece together. He saw Will walking from the house to the large old red barn behind it and decided to follow him. What better place to start learning about Jane than her father?

But as Allan entered the large, airy barn, which smelled sweetly of hay and dry feed and animal sweat, he couldn't see Will at first. Only a black-and-white spotted cow. The direct way the animal looked at him made him pause for a moment. It was almost as if they'd met somewhere before!

"That you, hon?" Will's throaty voice asked.

Allan laughed as Jane's father appeared from behind the animal. "Just me, sweetheart."

"C'mon over here, young man." Will smiled broadly, his old leathery face crinkling up. "I've been meaning to talk to you. You met Zelda yet?"

Allan came forward, stopping a few steps short of the suspiciously familiar beast. "I don't believe I've had the...pleasure."

They *had* met before. But where? And when?

"Old Zelda's the great-great-great granddaughter of the first cow I ever bought. Some honor, huh?" Will laughed. "But it was enough of an honor to keep her off the auction block when I sold out the rest of my stock and shut the dairy." His eyes narrowed and he darted a glance toward the open barn door. "Where's Jane?"

Allan shrugged. "Probably in the house, working...or cleaning. Though why she's doing that is beyond me." Allan laughed. "You must be the cleanest single man on earth. Your house is spick-and-span."

Will shrugged. "That was just because Jane's Aunt Katherine cleaned up for the wedding last—" Abruptly, he shut his mouth and began petting Zelda's neck.

"Wedding?" Allan asked, the hairs at his nape prickling with curiosity.

"Huh?" Will said. "Oh, just something a while back..."

His reticence on the topic made Allan suspicious. Had something happened with Jane? A disastrous marriage? It was apparently a subject her father didn't want to discuss.

He glanced down and could have sworn that cow was looking him straight in the eye. Almost as if she knew something he didn't. Something about this mysterious wedding?

Ridiculous! The crash had rattled his head, all right. If one strange glance from a cow could start him imagining things about secret weddings, his recovery must not be going very well. He lowered himself onto a hay bale.

"Nice place you have here," he told Will. "Jane told me you retired from the dairy business."

Will harrumphed. "I didn't want to, really, but Jane nagged at me so, she finally wore me down."

Allan shook his head. "If I were in the dairy business, I don't think I'd ever retire. I can't think of anything I'd like better than to live in the country, working with animals."

Will's forehead became a tangled mass of lines. *"You?"*

Good heavens. Did everyone think he was a citified workaholic sourpuss? "Sure, why not?"

"You ever live in the country?"

"Well..." Allan searched his memory, which came up blank, but doubtful. "I don't think so. But that doesn't mean I wouldn't like to. Lying in bed this morning, I came up with a dandy scheme for a place like this."

Will chuckled. "A scheme, huh? You should tell that to Jane. She'd feel a lot better if she knew you were scheming."

Allan shrugged. "Oh, I know she has some odd idea about my being different than I was, but honestly, I feel fine. She's probably just not used to seeing me at home, in bed."

Jane's father turned quickly away. "I wouldn't know about that."

"Once my arm heals, I'll be as good as new."

"Maybe so." He squinted at Allan, but it wasn't his arm he was inspecting; it was his head.

Even this good-tempered old man seemed skeptical when it came to his recovery. Allan was beginning to fear that he'd wake up someday and find that he had changed into a troll overnight. But apparently, that was what everyone else *wanted.*

"You know what this farm reminds me of?" Allan asked Will.

"No, what?"

"Ice cream."

Will looked surprised. "You don't say."

"Homemade ice cream."

"I do love homemade," Will agreed. "Haven't had it since I don't know when. But look here." He got up and practically loped over to a corner of the barn, where an old wooden ice-cream maker stood. He lifted it and blew off some of the inch or so of gathered dust. "Bet the thing still works!"

"Oh, sure," Allan agreed. He was almost as excited as Will. "Those old ones last forever."

"It's the crank kind—takes some elbow grease," Will said. "But with some fresh cream—"

"Do you have any good vanilla?"

"Vanilla!" Will scoffed. "We'll use rum, my boy!"

"*Dad!*"

Suddenly the two men turned and found Jane standing in the barn's entrance, one hand on her hip, the other stiffly at her side, holding a cordless telephone receiver.

"Allan should not be *drinking*," she said firmly.

"Aw, Janie, I wasn't talking about drinking rum, just using it in ice cream."

"Ice cream!" she said. "Allan doesn't like ice cream."

"Sure I do," Allan said.

She raised her eyebrows in surprise. "Well, you might *like* it, but you certainly don't eat it. It's practically one-hundred percent fat!"

"Of course," Allan said. "That's what makes it good."

Jane rolled her eyes, but abandoned the argument. "I have Grady Grimly on the phone, Allan."

Allan frowned, and looked longingly at that ice-cream maker, then at the phone. "Can you tell him I'll call back?"

She lifted the receiver and pressed the mute button. "You'll have to talk to your partner sometime, Allan. There was a notice in one of the papers today about your accident. He's very worried."

"Hadn't you already told him about it?"

"Grady never trusts anything till he reads it in the paper."

Allan flashed Jane a smile. "I promise, I'll call him this afternoon, later."

Jane stared at him a moment, transfixed, and the intense curiosity in those green eyes tugged at him. Why did he sometimes catch her staring at him so strangely?

For a brief moment, he remembered what she had told him about Grady Grimly's wanting to marry her, and it made him nervous. Had she ever considered accepting the proposal? Her father had mumbled something about a wedding...which made him wonder. The house had been cleaned for a wedding. Her father had been slipping him pieces of white cake that looked suspiciously like a wedding cake. And why had he been driving to Vermont in the first place?

Had Jane been on the verge of marrying Grady?

Just the idea made him panicky—just as he'd felt when she'd been talking about Clyde Simington and blushed—but he tried to keep smiling. It was only a suspicion.

Jane's brow wrinkled a little bit more. "All right, if you're sure..."

"I'm sure," he said, then took a few steps toward

her. "Here, these are for you." He held out the little bouquet he had picked for her, which was already looking a little wilted.

Jane stared at the thing as though it were a handful of poison ivy. "I can't take those," she said.

"Why not? Is there something else I've forgotten— like your having an allergy to wildflowers?"

"No, it's just—"

"Aw, take 'em, Janie," her father said.

She did, carefully avoiding touching fingers with Allan. For a few moments, she stood in front of them, silently holding the flowers in one hand and the phone in the other, looking miserable, her pale cheeks tinged with pink. Then she shot a suspicious glance between Allan and her father, turned and strode back to the house.

Allan couldn't quite take his eyes off her retreating back as she walked to the house with the phone. She was so tall, so graceful as the light wind nipped at her slender form. And the way her jeans hugged her hips and legs was enough to...

Behind him, Will cleared his throat. Allan turned, and didn't miss the amused glint in the older man's clear blue eyes as Will reminded him, "I believe we were talkin' about ice cream?"

Allan smiled. "Ice cream, yes."

But he could think of something much sweeter. Like Jane's lips, and the prospect of kissing her again. Soon.

ICE CREAM! All afternoon her father and Allan had been running around the kitchen like two kids, standing over their wooden caldron of cream, sugar and rock salt, mixing up frozen concoctions like two sorcerers with sweet tooths.

Jane just didn't understand where she had gone wrong. She'd been so certain she could bring Allan's memory back with her barrage of work, but the man had turned ornery on her. Genial, but ornery. He wasn't reading the papers, he hadn't made a business call since his accident, and the only time she'd caught him on the computer, he'd been playing Tic-Tac-Drop. And now this—ice cream and flowers!

He was getting further and further away from his old self, not closer. After leaving the two in the barn earlier she had conferred with Dr. McGillicutty over the phone and learned that it couldn't possibly be his medication that was turning him into this flirting, winking, ice-cream-concocting charmer.

When it came to handling this new Allan, she was at a complete loss. And the fact that she couldn't seem to get control of the situation made her angry. Allan *would* turn nice just when she wanted to be mean to him!

"Wanna try the raspberry?"

The enthusiastic voice behind her almost made her topple off the couch. When she pulled her gaze away from the evening news and turned, Allan was grinning like mad and holding a spoon with a creamy pink dollop on it. His other arm in its sling lent him a rather rakish, Napoleonic stance.

"We just made this," he explained, inching the spoon closer to her.

She allowed herself to be caught in the web of his handsome gaze only for a few moments before she ducked her head away. "No thank you."

He looked crestfallen—just as he had when she'd turned down his chocolate and rum raisin flavors earlier in the afternoon. "Don't you like raspberry, either?"

"I'm not particularly fond of ice cream at all," she replied. "And what's more important, neither are you."

"Me?" he asked innocently. "That's ridiculous! I'm crazy about the stuff. You would be, too, if you gave it half a chance." He sent her one of those grins that made her feel as if she'd melt faster than the scoop of ice cream he kept moving ever closer to her lips.

But of course she was just being silly, weak. She wasn't attracted to Allan anymore. Not after what he had done to her!

She took a deep, fortifying breath. "I don't want—"

Before she could get her sentence out, however, Allan slipped the spoon between her lips and she found herself wrapping her taste buds around a flavorful explosion of sugar and berries and cream.

"Mmmm," she said, swallowing. She couldn't help herself, any more than she could stop the smile that touched her lips. "That's good!"

He nodded. "Told you so," he taunted, vaulting the couch easily and landing smack-dab next to her. "Now what's this about me not liking ice cream?"

God, he was sexy. There was just no denying it. She could barely look at the man without thinking about how handsome he was, how wonderful it had felt to be in those arms, to run her hands across the wide expanse of his chest. To kiss him.

She swallowed, still tasting the sweet, rich flavor of the ice cream. "You don't," she informed him. "Do you realize how bad that stuff is for you?"

Distractedly he shook his head, then darted out a hand to tuck away a maverick strand of hair that had escaped the confines of her navy-blue headband. Jane ducked her head, but not soon enough to avoid feeling his hand against the sensitive flesh of her earlobe.

He chuckled. "I didn't think it was health food."

She sighed. The old Allan wouldn't have considered putting anything past his lips that wasn't healthy. Maybe that was the problem. Maybe the old Allan was gone. Permanently. What if the doctor was wrong and that person she had known for so many years, had idolized and even loved before she'd come to her senses, what if he was gone?

She felt an inexplicable surge of emotion. How would she ever bring her relationship with him to any kind of completion if he just disappeared? She would never have the pleasure of telling him off, of explaining that *she* had decided that marriage to him was the last thing on earth she wanted. She wasn't a person normally given to vengeance. But would she go the rest of her life, never able to put Allan in his place for his cavalier treatment of her?

She felt like shaking the man in front of her, and would have, if she'd thought she could somehow jar his memory back into place. If only she could just tell him the truth outright.

"Jane..."

She felt Allan tug on her hand and looked up at him warily. She didn't know if she had the willpower to dodge any more kisses this afternoon. In fact, she felt the most perverse desire to hop on top of Allan and give *him* a kiss that would shock him right out of his sneakers.

Which only proved that Allan might have lost his memory, but *she* was clearly losing her mind!

He cleared his throat. "Jane?"

She blinked, tried but failed to retrieve her hand and smiled tensely. "Yes?"

He appeared hesitant. "There's something I think I should tell you. Something rather important."

His voice was grave, with the same tone he usually used for referring to the crash of eighty-seven.

"I think I should tell you that I know about your little secret."

Jane swallowed. Oh, no. Had her father told him?

Still, she managed to croak out "S-secret?"

He smiled patiently. "The wedding," he told her. "It wasn't that hard to guess, you know."

She was sure she went red all over. Her father *must* have told him! And what was she going to do now? He was looking on her so pityingly, it would be especially hard to double back and tell him that she wasn't an object to be pitied, that *he* was, since she had decided that she didn't want to marry him anyway.

Oh, great. Now all her plans had been muffed. She couldn't wait to give her father a good talking-to for this!

Allan squeezed her hand a little more tightly, which just made her want to scream. "You're too good for him, Jane."

That was the truth! She remembered the old Allan, the bitter disappointment she had felt on the day of her wedding, and fumed anew at how gullible she'd been, how foolishly mistaken to anchor her dreams to a man who cared more for his car than any person.

And then she looked up at Allan, who was staring at her so earnestly. So innocently. So cluelessly.

This man didn't know what the heck he was talking about.

"Allan, about this wedding..." she began gingerly. She didn't want to give too much away before she knew what he was thinking. "I believe you have some of the details confused."

No emotional shocks... The doctor's words rang mockingly in her ears. Of course she couldn't tell him outright. But if Allan just happened to guess...well, she couldn't be held accountable for things beyond her control.

"What details?" he asked.

"Well, for instance, the small matter of the groom..."

"You don't have to name names, Jane," he assured her.

"Allan—"

"Believe me," he continued, not letting her get a word in edgewise, "you did the right thing. Exactly the right thing. Whoever he is, you can do better. You might feel lonely now, but—"

"Allan," she said more forcefully. His condescension was more than a little irksome. She would have liked to tell him that that was precisely the reason she had decided not to marry him. Because she could do better for herself and her baby.

"You're a bright woman, Jane," he bumbled on. "A little on the serious side, maybe, but I just know that someday—"

This was too much! *Her,* serious? That was fine talk coming from the man who had been named after a mean fish. "You can just stop right there, Mr. Sunshine. You've got it all wrong."

At her outraged tone, he did stop, in midsentence, looking so nonplussed that Jane was tempted to laugh. "I do?"

She crossed her arms over her chest and gritted her teeth, not caring if Dr. McGillicutty tarred and feathered her for what she was about to do. "*You* were the groom, Allan. The day you had your car accident was supposed to be your wedding day."

But Jane felt a flush of guilt upon seeing the confusion that crossed over Allan's face. No emotional shocks, the doctor had cautioned. Allan dropped her hand abruptly and stared at her, completely perplexed. She wasn't sure what would happen next, though she half expected him to suddenly start twitching and contorting, morphing back into his former self like something out of an old Jekyll and Hyde movie.

Instead, he remained perfectly still, staring at her with the same look of disbelief.

Every sound in the house seemed amplified—the ticking of the old grandfather's clock, her father's whistling coming from the kitchen, the monotonously perky tone of the anchor on the evening news. Had she just made a terrible mistake, damning Allan to a lifetime of memory oblivion?

All at once, the voice coming from the television changed from male to female. A very familiar female. Both Jane and Allan swung their heads around to face the set, and found themselves staring into the perfectly made-up visage of Patricia Blakemore, standing on a windswept beach in a raincoat, mike in hand.

"A few years ago the poor condition of America's beaches launched a surge of protest...."

A surge of protest seemed to rush through Jane's veins as she stared at the picture-perfect sight Patricia Blakemore created on that stretch of beach. What was *she* doing here? she wondered helplessly. She had assumed that Patricia was still in Paris with her latest *amour*.

"My God," Allan breathed, never taking his eyes off Patricia.

Slowly, Jane turned to him, feeling a prickly dart of envy at the reverential way he stared at the television, almost consumed by the sight of Patricia. It was as if he had forgotten that Jane existed.

"We were going to be married, weren't we?" he asked in a hushed voice.

Jane swallowed. That, of course, was what she had been trying to tell him, but now it struck her that Allan wasn't referring to her; he was still gazing straight at Patricia. His *ex*-bride to be.

And gazing at her so lovingly that Jane had to bite her tongue from making a tart response. For some irritating, inexplicable reason, it hurt that the first person to jar Allan's memory was Patricia, not her.

Suddenly, her plan to dump Allan—the old Allan—seemed so futile. Even if she could retrieve him out of this new, nicer incarnation, he so obviously didn't care a fig about her. What would it matter to him if Jane did decide to dump him? He was still much more upset about losing Patricia than he would ever be about her.

She crossed her arms, trying to physically keep at bay the empty feeling rising inside her. If Allan truly loved Patricia after everything he'd been through, Jane had a perfect opportunity right here and now to exact an even better form of revenge.

She fashioned her lips into what she hoped was a kindly, condescending smile. "Yes, Allan," she told him solemnly, "that's Patricia Blakemore. Your ex-fiancée."

"Patricia." He repeated the name that apparently was not at all familiar to him, then turned to Jane. "What happened?"

This was the part where she finally got to stick the knife in and give it a little twist. "You were going to be married, but at the last minute, she ran off to Paris with the president of her network."

His mouth popped open, and he turned to take another look at the woman who had treated him so badly. At that moment, Patricia was going on about some smart city fathers in one town who had solved the problem of dirty beaches by simply paving the beach over and turning it into extra parking for nearby strip malls.

Jane knew she should be happy when she saw the two red stains appear in Allan's cheeks, and the hooded anguish in his eyes, but unfortunately, revenge wasn't as sweet as was often claimed.

"Was I...I mean, were we..." He was so flummoxed that he couldn't finish his sentence.

Jane nodded. "You were terribly in love with her, Allan." Then, unable to keep the truth from leaping out, she added, "I think you still are."

He shook his head. "I don't know...this is such a shock. I mean, it's so sudden."

"Yes, I suppose it does seem fresh to you." Seeing Allan suffer twice for Patricia's crime of the heart wasn't nearly as satisfying as she had hoped it would be.

"If it all happened last week, why wouldn't it be fresh?"

Jane sucked in a breath. *Last week?*

Of course! Allan had no way of knowing that he had been at the center of two calamitous weddings.

"But why would I be getting married in Vermont?" he asked.

Jane couldn't let him go on like this. "Because it's

my house, Allan,'' she said, intending to explain it all to him in full.

He nodded and jumped in, saying, "I see. Your father was going to let us have this rustic house for our wedding. That was very nice of him.''

"Allan, I don't think you—"

He held up his hand. "No, don't," he said. "I understand everything now. You've been more than kind, but you don't have to keep on. You've been so uncomfortable around me, and now I see why. I must have just found out about Patricia's running away just before the wedding, and I was on my way to tell you it was called off.... Or did that all happen before?''

Jane felt numb. "Yes, before.''

"Ah, then I was coming here as a kind of retreat.''

"Allan—''

He took her hand again, smiling apologetically. "I've been wondering why you and your father have been watching me so oddly. Gosh, you must have thought I was an idiot, flirting with you this way when you knew all along I was brokenhearted.''

"Allan, if you'd just let me get a word in—''

But this time it wasn't Allan who interrupted her, it was the doorbell. Rolling her eyes impatiently, Jane strode to the front door and flung it open.

At first, as she looked at the woman standing on the other side of the threshold, she was certain she must be seeing things. But when she blinked the image didn't go away—no matter how hard she wanted it to.

In front of her stood Patricia Blakemore, in the perfectly tanned flesh. But how could she be on TV and here at the same time?

Before Jane could even work up the spit to say any-

thing to her, the woman had spotted Allan on the couch
and almost flattened Jane in her rush to get to him.

Jane scurried after the beautiful blonde, nearly choking in her perfume-drenched wake. She felt she should
warn Patricia, to stop her from saying anything that
might make things more confused than they already
were.

But before she could catch up with Patricia, much
less take her aside for a word or two, the woman had
dropped to her knees and sprawled herself gracefully
across Allan's lap.

"Darling!" she cried, looking up at him with sincere,
liquidy eyes. "I've come back to you, Allan, and this
time nothing will ever part us!"

Allan's confused gaze seemed pinned by Patricia's
for a long moment before he finally glanced up at Jane,
seeking help.

But that was something she wasn't about to give him.
When she'd first seen Patricia at the door she'd wanted
to hide her from Allan. Yet just looking at the lovers'
reunion made her put her own jealousy aside. For days
she had been hoping to find a way to give Allan the
grief he'd deserved for what he'd done to her.

Now, she realized, he'd just gotten it. In spades.

Chapter Four

Allan stared back down at Patricia's perfectly coiffed blond hair in utter confusion. First he never knew she existed, then he learned he had loved and lost her, and now he had her back—all in the span of about three minutes.

But did he actually want her?

Patricia. Patricia… He kept thinking the name to himself, over and over, trying to feel some connection to it. Of course, he must care a great deal for the woman who was draped across his lap so emotionally. No Tony-winning actress had ever looked so heart-torn and remorseful, no opera diva could have imbued so much depth into her voice when she'd said, "Nothing will ever part us!" And when he'd first seen Patricia on the television screen, he'd felt a jolt similar to the one he'd experienced when Jane had told him his Mercedes had been totaled. But right now all he felt was confusion—and slight nausea from Patricia's overly sweet perfume.

Seeking some kind of aid, he looked across the room to Jane. Biting her lip, she looked equally thrown off-kilter by their unexpected visitor. Equally nauseated, even.

"Patricia," he muttered, trying to pry the woman off

his leg, to which she was attached more tightly than a snail to a rain barrel. "Patricia, how did you get here so fast?"

"What?"

"You were just on television."

"Oh, that was the first of the new taped segments I'm doing. How did I look?"

"Fine..." Allan shook his head, still trying to figure this all out. "How did you know I would be here?"

She looked up at him with beautiful round blue eyes. "There was a notice in the paper, and then I spoke with Grady."

Having failed utterly to get her off him, Allan crossed his good arm over his sling and regarded her suspiciously. "And whatever happened to Mr. Network?"

Patricia blinked defensively, as if he was being somehow unreasonable to bring up the fact that she had run off with another man. "Tony?" she asked. "That's all over with. That's why I had to come see you. I realized right away that I made a terrible mistake, and now it's over."

"This Tony person, does he think it's over?"

"Of course!" Patricia said. "I do think he loved me, but he had a network to run, and of course, there was his wife to consider."

Allan fell back against the cushions in shock. "His *wife?*"

Patricia nodded. "Can you believe that woman had the nerve to sneak all the way to Paris to spy on us?" She let out a huff of disgust. "Well, she just showed the poorest taste. But after some thought, Tony and I decided it would be best if we didn't let our personal feelings interfere with our careers."

"How mature of you," he observed.

She looked confused. "Maybe you didn't catch my drift, sweetheart. I've come back to you—and I still have my job. You might say I even got a promotion. In fact, you just saw it. Instead of that drab old morning show, Tony's giving me a taped spot on the nightly newscast. We're going to call it 'America Alive!' and it will be all about trends—you know, so everyone out there will know what's going on in the good old U.S. of A."

Allan looked up and noted that Jane was having a hard time hiding a wry grin. "How nice of you news-people in New York to fill us in," she said.

Her sarcasm sailed smoothly over Patricia's head. "Oh, people just love soft news," she said, nodding in agreement.

Allan cleared his throat. "Well, Patricia, I'm not sure about all of this."

Her brow wrinkled. "But aren't you happy about my job? I'll be making more money, too, naturally."

"Yes, that's wonderful...." He wasn't sure how to put this. It was as though she didn't even expect him to be the slightest bit angry that she had run off to Paris with a married man in lieu of marrying him. "But you have to realize, Patricia, things have changed."

He noticed Jane start creeping toward the door, and beckoned her to stay. Without Jane, he wasn't certain he would know how to react to any other bombshells Patricia might lob his way. No matter how hard he racked his brains, he barely understood the circumstances of all this; he felt like an actor forced to impro-vise while the rest of the cast worked from a full script.

Seeing the pleading glance he sent Jane, Patricia nar-rowed her gaze on her, too. "Oh. Grady had said some-thing about..."

She stopped and gave Jane a thorough once-over, from her hair pulled back in a simple drugstore barrette to the old worn-out tennis shoes on her feet. Then, apparently satisfied that she didn't have anything to worry about from the competition here, she looked back at Allan, smiling more confidently. "But never mind—what's past is past. Now that we're together again, I'm not going to let you out of my sight even for an itty-bitty minute! In fact, as soon as you can pack, I'm taking you back to the city with me and giving you more TLC than you've ever had in your life."

"Oh, dear," Allan muttered.

His words caused her to flop against him once more in a dramatic display that would have put Tallulah Bankhead to shame. "It's so wonderful to hear you call me 'dear' again!"

"But—"

In the corner, Jane giggled. "Allan, if you won't be needing me…"

"But I *do* need you," he said, hoping his gaze conveyed his desperation.

He just didn't understand it. At first when Jane had seen Patricia he could have sworn she wanted to scratch the woman's eyes out, but now she appeared almost gleeful at the difficulty he was having extracting himself from her embrace.

"Why?" Jane asked.

"For one thing," he said, "we need to explain to Patricia here that I couldn't possibly go back to Manhattan right now."

"Really?" Jane asked, all innocence. "Why not?"

"Because I'm an invalid, darn it!" he cried in frustration.

Patricia looked up, her blue eyes dripping with concern. "But of course you are, darling. That's why we need to get you back to civilization, to some real doctors."

"Dr. McGillicutty is a real doctor," Allan said, annoyed by her high-handed tone. Annoyed by *her*.

He couldn't believe it. Was he really in love with this woman? She was lovely, of course, but...

But so was Jane. And with the other woman watching, he found himself wanting to push Patricia away, preferably all the way back to Manhattan, so he could have some more time to get to know Jane. But apparently that wasn't going to happen. Not with the blonde sticking to him like a barnacle.

The barnacle giggled. "Oh, Allan. Dr. McGillicutty? Even the name sounds like some country quack."

He glanced up at Jane, whose lips were twisted into the same rigid line that his were. "Tell her, Jane. Didn't the doctor say I shouldn't be moved?"

For a moment, Jane looked torn, but she finally admitted, "Yes, I guess he did."

He felt his body sag in relief, especially when he detected a trace of defeat in Patricia's blue eyes. "I see," she said.

The hurt tone in her voice softened him a little. "I'm sorry you came out all this way, Patricia."

She blinked. "Why?"

He shrugged. "Well, because..." Because he felt that somehow, even though he was supposedly in love with her, he could have whiled away the rest of his life quite happily without seeing her again. "For one thing, you've gone to a lot of trouble getting here...."

More trouble, apparently, than she went to on the day they were supposed to be married.

Finally, Patricia stood. "Well, of course!" she cried, laughing. "You're my fiancé!"

Allan bristled. "Patricia, there's one thing we need to get straight."

"I agree," she said resolutely. "First, I need to know where to put my things."

"Things?"

"I didn't bring much. Except for my makeup case, naturally. You know I never go anywhere without *that*. As for the rest, I'll just have to go into town and outfit myself for a week in the country."

Panic surged through him. "You can't stay here!" He tried to stand, too, but without his other arm to help push himself up, he found himself buried in the deep, comfy cushions of the couch. He turned to Jane for help. "Tell her, Jane. There's not enough room here."

Jane looked from Allan to Patricia and back again. "Oh, we've got plenty of rooms," she said, though her tone didn't reveal much eagerness to have Patricia as a permanent addition to their household.

"But the imposition," Allan said, his voice growing more desperate. "You haven't even met Jane's father," he told Patricia.

"I wouldn't be any trouble at all," Patricia said dismissively. "In fact, I could be a big help. I'll bet you didn't know that when I was a little girl, I wanted to be either a newswoman or a nurse."

The mental image of Patricia as a real nurse, facing off with bandages and bedpans, was enough to garner a laugh from Jane. She glanced over at Allan, a spark of mischief in her eyes. "Dad wouldn't mind more company, Allan. You know that. And after all, what better person to nurse you back to your old self than your *fiancée?*"

He didn't trust the evil gleam in her eye when she said that.

"That's settled then," Patricia announced. "I'm staying here to take care of you, and that's all there is to it!"

Jane smiled brightly. Too brightly. "I'll go get Dad," she said.

Allan made one last struggle to wrest himself from the overstuffed couch, but ended up flopping back in defeat.

Once Jane was out of the room, Patricia turned to him with a big smile. "Isn't this wonderful? We're together again, just like it was meant to be."

"Listen, Patricia—"

In a split second, she was on the couch next to him, her arms draped about his shoulders. Her voice dropped into pouty babytalk. "Is my sweet little snooky still mad at his Patty-boo?"

Allan rolled his eyes. As if being dumped at the altar was a thing a person just got over in the blink of an eye.

She narrowed her eyes and waggled a perfectly manicured finger at him. "Now, admit it," she cooed. "I know you're still an itsy-bitsy bit angry."

"Patricia, I just don't know what to say. Maybe you aren't aware of this, but I can't even remember all that went on between us now."

She shook her head, laughing, and Allan couldn't help noticing that when she did so, not a hair on her head moved. Her blond locks were so heavily sprayed it was as if the individual hairs had all been fused together. "Oh, I don't believe that!"

"But it's true," he said.

"Are you saying that you don't remember me?"

He looked at her doubtfully. "To be honest, not really."

She smiled, showing her full line of expensively acquired straight white teeth, then dropped down next to him, slinking against him seductively. "Then I'll give you something that will bring it all back to you."

Before he could push away, Patricia's lips were smack against his. It was such a sneak attack that he simply felt he was drowning in perfume and hairspray, pinned down by two sets of nails filed to razor sharpness digging into his shoulders.

On the other side of the room someone cleared his throat. Allan extricated himself enough from Patricia's lips to look up and see Jane and Will, staring at the two of them entwined together. Patricia let out a dissatisfied little moan at the interruption that made Allan wince. Both of his hosts looked pale, almost sickly.

But Jane bounced back quickly. Her wan complexion soon had a high color—but even so, Allan was sure he was more red-faced than she. He couldn't believe the way Patricia had pounced on him the moment they were left alone in the room. The woman was faster than a mongoose.

"Dad," Jane said, her tone tight and businesslike, "this is Patricia Blakemore. She'll be staying with us for a few days. You might recognize her from the news."

A hint of recognition lit in Will's eyes. "Oh, sure."

"Patricia is Allan's fiancée." Jane shot her father a look, the meaning of which Allan couldn't decipher.

Slowly, Will turned his gaze back to their new visitor. He looked Patricia up and down then and nodded at her with uncharacteristic curtness. "Welcome."

"Why thank you," Patricia said. "I just know I'll have Allan up and running in no time."

This bold statement of purpose produced a wry smile from their host. Will crossed his arms in a stance that mirrored Jane's. "From the looks of things when we came in here, I'd say you're already doing a fair job of revving his engine."

"Oh, I'm just exhausted!"

Jane looked up in time to see Patricia sink gracefully into a chair. Dressed in a formfitting denim skirt and matching jacket, with a low-cut top peeking through, she looked more like a Gap ad than the nurse she claimed to be. Her makeup, as always, was perfect, and not a hair on her head was out of place.

Jane had been busy all morning cooking and getting the house in order, but she *looked* like it. Even now she was certain her face was red and her hair drooped more than usual from standing over the stove cooking lunch. She couldn't imagine what Patricia had been doing to leave her so tuckered out and yet so immaculate. "Has Allan been running you ragged?"

Patricia raised one meticulously plucked eyebrow high on her forehead. "I've never stared at so many numbers since the week I had to read the business news on WNYZ."

Jane looked at her suspiciously. "Allan's been looking at numbers?" This was news.

"Of course!" Patricia said. "You know Allan. Everything's work, work, work with that man."

"Really?" For all her trying, she hadn't been able to get him to do a thing.

Patricia nodded. "Of course, I told him that what he was asking me to do would be more appropriate for *you.*

That is, if you *are* still working under Allan." Patricia sent her a disapproving glare. "Grady told me something about...well, a slight indiscretion between you and Allan."

Jane felt ire rising inside her. Patricia was a fine one to talk about indiscretions! "That's all over now."

"Oh, my dear, I was certain it was. Clearly Allan was just on the rebound from me."

It took every ounce of strength for Jane not to have a serious bean accident with Patricia's camera-perfect hair. Unfortunately, there was an undeniable truth in the newswoman's words. "I think I should tell you," she said, in the interest of keeping things straight. "Allan doesn't remember that he was going to marry me."

Patricia nodded sagely. "I did a story once on trauma cases. They say victims usually only remember the important things."

Jane couldn't have explained why such a lame dig stung so much. "Really? How interesting. Allan didn't remember a single thing about you, either," she couldn't help informing the woman. "I even had to point you out on the news yesterday."

Maybe the barb was a mistake. Patricia's lips thinned determinedly, and her eyes looked as if they could have shot daggers. "I don't care what you think of me or what I've done. I'm in love with Allan, and I always have been."

"Even when you trotted off to Paris?"

Patricia balled her fists at her sides and huffed in frustration. "Oh, am I going to have to hear about that one tiny slip forever? Look, I found Allan first. He's mine."

To her, it was that simple. She needed a man, and Allan was the most obvious choice she could think of.

"You're welcome to him," Jane said. "I wouldn't have him on a platter."

Patricia smirked. "You're a smart girl to take that attitude. For one thing, you and Allan are nothing alike. Allan likes a woman with ambition, money and style. Did you know that I get my hair done by the same woman who does Katie Couric?"

Jane couldn't think of a thing to say except, "Oh, really?"

Patricia rose with a swagger, as if she felt she had just scored big. "I'm going to town to buy Allan's papers now. Although I would think that would be *your* job, too."

"I'll be glad to buy them," Jane said.

Patricia held her hand palm out. "No, Allan specifically asked *me* to do it. He said the drive would do me good. You see, even though he's sick himself, the dear man is still more concerned about my welfare."

Jane smiled. There was probably more self-interest in Allan's attempt to get rid of Patricia than the woman was willing to realize. "How sweet."

Satisfied that she had come out on top in the argument, Patricia flitted out the door, and Jane turned back to her stove, brooding. She didn't know how she was going to survive another day with that woman—much less the three days until Allan's next doctor appointment, when Dr. McGillicutty might give him the okay to return to Manhattan.

One thing she was sure of, however. The more time she spent around Patricia, the more certain she was that the beautiful blonde was exactly the vengeance on Allan she had been seeking. Especially since poor Allan apparently couldn't remember what would have attracted him to Patricia in the first place. It was like John Boy

Walton waking from a deep sleep to discover he was engaged to Cruella de Vil.

She giggled. Despite the residual pangs of envy she sometimes felt around the two of them, the trouble was worth it. With time—hopefully some time soon—she wouldn't care a fig about the entire situation. Allan would be firmly saddled with the woman he deserved, and she would be able to push on to more important matters.

She had a baby to think of. A baby to name. In her idle moments, Jane had already considered giving him or her a name with a financial flavor, since, in essence, this was going to be a child of Wall Street. Like Morgan, or Andrew Carnegie—names that had a lucky money aura. Rockefeller Fielding. Or how would Bill Gates Fielding sound? Going for the purely intellectual, she could call him Milton Friedman Fielding, though Milton might be a tough moniker to live down on the playground. Or, adding a showbiz touch, she could always name him Louis Rukeyser Fielding, after that silver-haired "Wall $treet Week" stalwart who had been on PBS since the Stone Age. Mr. Charisma himself! And that way, if she had a girl, she could be Louise Rukeyser Fielding.

Her fanciful thoughts were interrupted by the sound of the bell she had given Allan to ring in case of emergencies. He had never used it before, but now the thing was ringing like crazy. Jane's heart leaped into her throat. What could have happened?

She hit the kitchen door running. In all the hoopla over Patricia, she had forgotten that Allan was actually a sick person. She kicked herself for leaving his care to Patricia.

She skidded into his room, afraid she might find him

on the floor, unable to get up. Instead, he sat in the rocking chair in the corner, a big grin on his face. The silver emergency bell rested on the windowsill next to him.

Jane, who had already broken into a nervous sweat, stood panting in the center of the room. "What happened?" she asked.

"Nothing. I was bored."

She could have strangled him for scaring her like that! "Oh, honestly, Allan—Patricia's only been gone a few minutes."

"Actually, not even a minute. Her car just pulled out when I rang the bell, and you made it over here in nothing flat."

He grinned at her—as though there was something telling in the speed with which she responded to his fake emergency! "I thought something had happened to you."

"And that upset you?"

"Of course!"

This news seemed to please him.

Jane crossed her arms and took on a stern expression. "Now look here, Allan. I'm not going to let myself be wedged between you and Patricia."

"Wedge away," he encouraged.

"Allan!"

His expression took on a pout. "I doubt Patricia would give you an inch, anyway. This is the first moment of peace I've had since she arrived. She's always around, and the few times when she's not, there's still a pall over the room. Will came up this morning, but couldn't stay because he said he was choking from the smell."

Jane sniffed. There *was* a decided sweet, lingering scent in the air.

"This morning I asked her what the name of her perfume was, and she said it was called Unforgettable," Allan said.

"Very appropriate."

He laughed. "Well, it's true—for the perfume, at least."

She watched him carefully for a moment. Even after a day with Patricia, Allan hadn't changed. Jane had been certain that Patricia's arrival was bound to bring back something of the old Allan, who was still nowhere in existence.

Could it be that person was simply gone for good?

She didn't know whether she should be happy or sad at this thought, but as she stared into Allan's handsome face, she did know one thing. Patricia's showing up when she did was pure providence. A few more days alone in the house with Allan and his constant flirtation and, yes, Jane grudgingly admitted, his irresistible sexiness, and she might have been worn down. Might have forgotten all her prior plans, her determination to go it alone. And the hurt she had suffered at Allan's hands.

"Isn't Patricia even a small reminder of your old self, Allan?"

She could have sworn she saw a little shiver go through him. "Honestly, it doesn't seem that we have much in common."

"But—"

He laughed again. "You seem awfully eager to hook the two of us up."

"You just don't know how much she really means to you."

"How much?" Allan asked.

She didn't want to tell him all the heartache he went through after Patricia's defection. To do so would mean having to reveal that Patricia had run off to Paris last month, not just last week. "A lot," she said, knowing she was speaking nothing but the depressing truth. "Take my word for it."

He clearly didn't. Instead, he stood and came up to her, standing mere inches away. It was as if there were a force field between the two of them—a force fueled by pure physical attraction. She mentally braced herself against its pull, telling herself that *physical* attraction was all there was between them. And that was probably a mere residue of what she had once felt for Allan. She'd heard of amputees who could still feel lost limbs ache. Maybe this was something similar—desire as a phantom pain.

Allan's gray eyes zoomed in on her. "Do you mean that if I were back to what you so often refer to as 'my normal self,' I would take Patricia back?"

It took only a moment's hesitation for her to know what answer she had to give. "In a heartbeat."

Who knew but that the two of them might have gotten back together anyway? Even if Jane had married Allan, it was entirely possible that Patricia would have sailed into Allan's life again and taken upon herself the role of "other woman." Just thinking of that possibility was confirmation enough that Jane was doing the right thing for herself and her baby. A divorce was not something she wanted to go through.

She bit back a chuckle of irony. She and Allan had never even reached the altar, but in her mind she already had them battling each other in family court.

Allan looked disappointed. He took a step back, contemplating her words. "Then you think I shouldn't tell Patricia to go away?"

Jane pursed her lips. "I don't think she would even if you told her to."

He ran a hand through his thick dark hair in frustration. "Darn it, though, it's not Patricia I want. Can't you see—"

Jane darted away from his outstretched arm and cut him off before he could go any further. "You don't know what you're saying, Allan."

He regarded her in silence for a moment, his look so intense that she almost squirmed. "It's Grady, isn't it?"

"What?"

Allan nodded, as though her confusion were somehow a confirmation of his off-the-wall hunch. "I spoke with my partner this morning. He seemed more interested in your well-being than mine."

Jane winced. She had told Grady very little about this weekend—only that the wedding hadn't taken place and that he wasn't to speak to Allan about it. She hadn't wanted Grady pressing his suit again and making things more complicated than they already were. Now she wondered if there could be any way to avoid it.

"He seemed especially interested when I told him Patricia was here. I think he wants you back in New York."

"He probably was only interested in Patricia because he knows how strongly you feel about her."

"Felt," Allan corrected.

She tilted her head. "You can't know for certain that your love for Patricia is dead. At any rate, I don't think you should take any rash steps. What if you wake up tomorrow and discover you feel just like your old self and you're completely besotted with her?"

He smiled. "Are you trying to scare me?"

"I'm just warning you. You should never be too hasty. That's one of your mottoes, you know. 'Always keep an eye on your options. Never be too hasty.' You used to say that in business a person has three options— to plunge ahead, freeze or bail out. In this case, I would advise you to freeze."

He shook his head. "Of all those little nuggets of wisdom, I think I'd choose to bail."

"Then you'd be too hasty, and not keeping your options open."

He looked at her with a decidedly sexy sparkle in his eye. "Maybe I just prefer a different option."

His words made her heart slam to a standstill. Her tummy fluttered nervously when she looked up at him, but she fought against the feeling. She could not allow herself to become involved with this man again. Despite the obvious fact that he had hurt her, there were also too many unknowns in his life right now. She needed to create stability for herself and her child, not to hop on another emotional roller coaster with a man with no memory and a woman with no scruples.

She started edging back toward the doorway. "I'd better get back to my stove," she said, trying to hide the quaver in her voice.

"Must you?"

"Patricia will be back soon," she told him.

"Patricia again," he muttered, a boyish pout on his lips. Strange that even his good-humored petulance had a slightly sexy cast to it.

"Yes, Patricia," she affirmed. "If you're smart, you'll stick with her until you're more sure of yourself."

He grimaced. "And what if in two months I decide I still don't feel for her what I used to? What then?"

That was a good question. One Jane couldn't even begin to have an answer for. "Well then...you might talk to Grady."

Allan frowned, puzzled. "What could he do?"

"Give you the name of his psychiatrist."

"I'm serious," Allan said.

"All right," she answered. "You don't have to wait an eternity. Just until you're certain you would be acting out of real feeling, and not just from a bump on the head."

Suddenly, she heard footsteps behind her. She quickly turned, but instead of seeing Patricia, as she had expected, she saw her father. He patted her on the shoulder.

"Lunch is burning," he said. Jane jumped and was about to dash back to the kitchen when her father stopped her. "It's okay," he assured her. "I got it under control." Her father scratched his neck and regarded first her and then Allan. "You're usually so careful, though, I wondered what could have gotten you so fired up that you'd forget what you had on the stove. Now it all makes sense."

Jane looked around. "What do you mean?"

Her father laughed. "I heard that bell ring the second Barbara Walters pulled out of the drive."

"Dad!" Jane cried, horrified. "You shouldn't make insinuations like that. I gave that bell to Allan for emergencies!"

"That's right," Allan told him. "And my emergency was that I desperately needed someone to talk to me about something other than television news ratings."

"Well, never mind," Will went on. "I just came up to run an idea by you."

"Oh, not more about that ice-cream factory!" Jane moaned. The two of them had been floating the idea of starting up a little ice-cream works right here on the farm, an idea that sounded not only financially risky, but far too taxing for her father, whom it had taken her years to convince to retire.

But her father shook his head. "Nah," he said, dismissing her worries. "I thought it might be fun to plan a picnic."

His idea went over like a lead balloon. Jane couldn't see the "fun" of sitting around watching Patricia lounge on the grass with Allan. "Oh, Dad, do we have to?" she whined, knowing she sounded like a ten-year-old but unable to help herself.

Allan apparently didn't find the idea too appealing, either. He crossed his arms and repeated halfheartedly, "A picnic..."

Will cleared his throat. "There's a real nice spot on the other side of the lake. Real cozy. Secluded."

Jane immediately tried to picture what spot he had in mind, so it was a few moments before she looked up and discovered the two men exchanging meaningful glances...though just exactly what they meant she wasn't too sure.

She didn't trust them, though.

"A picnic," Allan repeated with growing enthusiasm, smiling broadly now as he rocked back on his heels. "What a wonderful idea!"

Chapter Five

"What do you think?"

Patricia twirled in her newest outfit, bought especially for the picnic. In the past days, Jane had learned the Patricia never went anywhere dressed inappropriately. The whole time she'd been in Vermont, she'd looked as if she were costumed for an assignment on rural life. And today, for the picnic, she looked...

Silly.

It was all Jane could do to hold back a laugh. The scoop-neck dress had a fitted bodice and a full skirt that was cut well above the knee, and was done in small blue checks. It might be something that a fourteen-year-old could pull off, but on a full-grown woman it looked a bit peculiar. Like something out of a Li'l Abner comic strip.

Jane took a deep breath. "It certainly is...eye-catching."

Detecting a certain lack of enthusiasm, Patricia flicked an annoyed glance her way. "Well, of course you wouldn't care for it. Anyone can tell that appearance isn't your number-one priority."

Jane looked down at her father's blue flannel shirt, which she was wearing untucked over another pair of jeans, and had to admit that she could hardly claim to be a fashion plate. But neither did she look ridiculous. "You know," she reminded Patricia, "we're going to be crossing the lake and eating on the grass."

"Well?" Patricia looked unfazed by the prospect.

"Oh, never mind," Jane said, realizing how futile it was to try to reason with someone who thought Connie Chung was as important a public figure as the President. "You look fabulous."

The empty compliment satisfied Patricia. "You're so sweet to say so," she cooed.

Jane had awakened that morning feeling sickly, especially at the prospect of going across a wavy lake to eat greasy, salty food. Now, dizzied by the tiny checks of Patricia's dress, she felt doubly ill. Having to watch Patricia prancing around in her Daisy Mae outfit, feeding Allan grapes in the great outdoors, wasn't going to settle her stomach.

By contrast, her father entered the kitchen with a bounce in his step. "Good news," he announced. "I just went down to the landing, and Art's got us two boats on reserve."

"You already rented them?" Jane asked. It was usually a lucky day when Art managed to rent any of his six boats.

"Of course," he answered, "we wouldn't want to have our plans foiled by a lack of transportation."

Jane had a hunch that her father and Allan were in cahoots about something. They had been having little private chats all day yesterday, and it was no secret that Patricia wasn't exactly her father's cup of coffee.

Will shrugged. "Well, if it were just us, naturally I wouldn't go to so much trouble. But I wouldn't want to take any chances with Miss Blakemore."

Patricia beamed at this royal treatment. "Please, don't do anything special on my account. Act just as you would if you didn't have a celebrity along."

Jane shot a glance at her father, whose lips were screwed up in a valiant effort to keep a straight face.

"We'll certainly try," he assured Patricia, "but... well, you must realize how difficult it is for us to forget that you're a television personality."

Especially since Patricia reminded them of that fact every fifteen minutes!

Patricia nodded, then turned to the door. "Oh! I think I hear Allan coming!"

Allan appeared a moment later, looking handsome and casual in a pair of khakis and a knit shirt. Jane recognized the shirt as one she had given her dad one Father's Day, though she somehow doubted he had even worn it. He was old-fashioned and stubbornly resisted wearing anything that wasn't cotton or wool broadcloth.

But Allan looked like a million bucks in it. The tighter-fitting cloth showed off just how well those afternoon bouts with the weight machines at his athletic club paid off. His arms, usually hidden beneath an Armani suit more completely than one was now hidden beneath a sling, bulged with muscles, and his broad chest appeared even broader than usual. Just to have spent an entire day standing in the kitchen looking at him would have been her idea of a picnic.

He answered her gawking stare with a wide grin. "Anything wrong, Jane?"

More than she could ever explain! She had no business staring at Allan that way. Darn it, why did he have to be so good-looking anyway?

"We'd better get moving," she said, shaking out of

her mind the memory of how it felt to be held in those arms of his.

"Are we on a schedule?" he asked, still grinning.

Her father let out a bark of a laugh. "Janie's always on a schedule. Likes things orderly, you know." He grabbed a basket of food and headed out before Jane could defend herself.

Not that she saw anything *wrong* with wanting things orderly.

"I'm not like that at all," Patricia said, looking a little miffed that Allan had acknowledged her presence with no more than a glance and a nod. "I just love doing things completely spur-of-the-moment."

Yeah, like running off to Paris with a married man.

Patricia twirled for Allan. "Just take this outfit. I saw it in town and I just thought it would be *perfect* for our little outing today—a little extravagant, of course. But like I always say, if I can't buy a few things, what's the point in making pots of money?"

Saying this, she batted her eyelashes at Allan; apparently, the idea that in his present amnesiac state he no longer cared about six-figure incomes had not yet sunk into Patricia's thick skull. Or maybe it was that armorlike layer of hairspray that made it so difficult for the idea to penetrate.

Neither of the men knew how to reply to this comment, so Jane's father said, "Shall we?" and gestured grandly toward the door.

Everything went smoothly for ten entire minutes...until they reached Art's boathouse.

There Jane discovered that her father had rented two very different kinds of boats: a spiffy motorboat and a leaky-looking rowboat.

"I'll take Miss Blakemore over in this baby," Will

announced, throwing two life preservers onto the sleek fiberglass motorboat. "Jane, you and Allan follow along."

As she stared from one man to the other, Patricia looked as panicked as Jane felt. "But don't you think I'd better go with Allan?" she asked.

Will grabbed Patricia's arm. "Just you step aboard, Miss Blakemore. I rented this one especially for you. Wouldn't want you to get your fetching new dress all mussed."

She looked torn, and turned to Allan for backup. "Darling...?"

Allan shrugged helplessly. "He *did* rent it for you especially."

"Come on, Miss Blakemore," Will said, tugging the blonde aboard.

Jane didn't like what was going on one bit. "Dad, wait. Maybe you and I—"

"I don't feel up to paddling, Janie. A little lumbago," he said with a grin.

Now Jane knew she had been set up. Lumbago? Her father never complained about his health. A moment later she heard him rev up his motor and saw him pull away from shore with Patricia. No wonder he'd looked so gleeful about renting the boats in advance. Allan had probably paid him to strand her with him on this slow-moving tub.

She turned to Allan. He stood next to the boat with the most innocent of expressions, smiling and waving to Patricia, who was quickly becoming just a blue-and-white-checkered shape.

"I bet you had a hand in this," Jane growled.

"Me?" he asked. "It was your father who rented our boats."

Jane picked up the oars and motioned for him to get into the rowboat. "Come on, Hiawatha. Let's see if we can get this thing across the lake."

"I'm sure you'll do fine," Allan said. When she sent him an inquiring glance, he pointed handily to his sprained arm.

Jane sighed and took her place in the back of the narrow, shaky vessel. Allan sat facing her—and away from the motorboat, which was speeding quickly toward the other shore. Much more quickly than their own torturous progress.

"Isn't this romantic?" Allan asked, taking a deep whiff of the clean country air.

Jane had already worked up a bit of a sweat, and they'd only gone twenty yards or so. "For you, maybe," she muttered. "To me it's like something out of the slave galley scene in *Ben Hur*."

He shot her one of those million-watt smiles of his that even after almost a week still caught her off guard. And probably always would.

Always, she amended, until she returned to Manhattan and found another job that wouldn't require her to see Allan Steele ever again.

"I thought you would appreciate getting out and dining alfresco."

"Oh, sure," she said, puffing. "I might enjoy having a heart attack alfresco, too."

He chuckled. "Then stop rowing so hard."

The boat that carried her father and Patricia was slowing down as it approached the opposite bank. "I'd like to reach the other side sometime before next year," she said.

"What's the hurry?" he asked.

Because the longer she sat in the boat with him, the

more she was taunted by the desire *not* to return to Manhattan. To simply stay forever in this peaceful little paradise, mooning into Allan's sexy eyes. Forget work. Forget the pertinent fact that in seven months she was going to have another mouth to feed.

That was the clincher. She *couldn't* forget that—even if Allan could. Or at least, he had apparently forgotten that they had done something that could conceive a child. At gut level, she still couldn't believe that was even possible. How could his mind have dismissed something that had seemed so earth-shattering to her?

How could he have forgotten that she'd actually told him she loved him?

Just thinking about it made her mad all over again and gave her a renewed burst of purpose. She started rowing even more determinedly. Suddenly the prospect of seeing Patricia fawning all over Allan seemed like just the dose of bad medicine she needed.

"Uh-oh," Allan said. "I don't think I like that look on your face."

She didn't reply.

He smiled, undaunted by her stony silence. "Has anyone ever told you that when you get frustrated, your chin sticks out?"

Jane nearly choked. What did he mean by that? "I think you're confusing frustration with fatigue."

He leaned back casually, studying her. "No, I think there's definitely something else at work here. And I've finally figured out what it is."

His knowing glance stopped her oars in midstroke. *Could he have guessed?*

He smiled. "It's Patricia."

Jane's mouth dropped open. "What?"

"I think you're a wee bit jealous of her."

Her jaw dropped. Jealous, of Patricia? Well, naturally she *did* feel a sort of envy toward the woman—but Allan's telling it to her face was too outrageous. "Do you expect us to get in a catfight over you?" she asked. "Because if that's what you're waiting for, I'm afraid you'll be very disappointed. On the contrary, I wish the two of you the greatest happiness."

"No, you don't," he said, smiling. "In fact, right now you look as though you wish us both at the bottom of this lake."

"Don't be silly."

"I'm just trying to figure you out."

Exhausted, Jane finally stopped to catch her breath, trying to ignore the swelling motion of the wavelets and its unsettling effect on her stomach. Trying to ignore Allan's handsome gaze and its infuriatingly potent effect on her senses. "There's nothing to figure out."

"Oh, yes, there is," he said, contradicting her.

"Come to think of it, I *am* tempted to take an oar and dump you overboard."

He ignored the gibe, following his own conversational bliss. "I keep wondering what makes you so prickly."

She stiffened. "I am not prickly."

"Hard to get, then," he said.

She nearly let out a rueful laugh. If only she'd played a little harder to get two months ago!

"Just look at the lengths I have to go to in order to kiss you," he said. "First I tried the sneak attack. Now it's getting us stranded in the middle of a lake."

Suddenly, she looked around and discovered that was exactly what she had allowed to happen. Her father's boat was on the other side of the lake already, a mere dot in the distance. And Allan was half standing in an attempt to edge closer to her in the wobbly boat.

"Are you insane?" she squeaked. "We'll capsize."

"Wouldn't it be worth it for a kiss?"

"No! Allan, you can't swim!"

This news appeared to surprise him. "Seriously?"

"Yes," she said. "So please be careful!"

"No problem."

He pointed proudly to the ancient orange life preservers they had rented from Art, and moved forward, nearly toppling out of the boat as they crossed the wake from a passing motorboat.

Jane groaned.

"You're the one who's making this so difficult," he argued.

She yelped as their vessel pitched to one side.

He braced his legs, perched to give the boat another tip. "Just one kiss?" he asked.

"Absolutely no—" He shifted his weight, sending the boat perilously off balance again. "All right!" she cried, relenting. "Just sit down!"

Unfortunately, he was close enough to plop himself down right next to her on the narrowed strip of wood that passed for a seat. "There," he said with a grin.

Jane sighed, gritting her teeth against the warmth that moved through her when their bodies made contact on the too-small bench, which bowed under their combined weight. Happily, the pitching had stopped.

As suavely as a teenager in the back seat of his dad's Monte Carlo, Allan snaked an arm around her waist. "I kept my promise," he said, reminding her that a kiss was a part of the bargain. "But then, don't I always?"

She slowly turned to look him in the face. *Don't get carried away,* she told herself, attempting to approach the upcoming kiss with a cool head. Luckily, his little remark about keeping his promises made it easier to harden her heart against him. *Didn't he always?*

A more logical question would be, *did he ever?*

She forced her lips into a frown. "I'm only doing this because I've been blackmailed."

He ducked his head and cast a dubious glance at her. "You haven't thought about kissing me since that morning in my room?"

"No," she said, but the lie was barely audible.

His eyes, so gray and mesmerizing, trapped her under their spell. She wanted to kiss him; at the same time, she wanted to shake him, to make him remember that he was Allan Steele, the man who had been caught fleeing their marriage ceremony not a week ago, the man responsible for her heartbreak, not to mention her father's wasted wedding cake. The old Allan would have jumped on the motorboat with Patricia, his true love, and left her behind, wet and bedraggled in his churning wake. He wouldn't be sitting practically in her lap, mooning at her so believably that she was tempted to forget all about the hurt of just a week ago and throw herself in his arms.

"I think about kissing you all the time," Allan told her. "For instance, this morning, when you were watching me in the kitchen."

"Maybe you should have thought about kissing someone else. For instance, Patricia."

He shook his head in mock wonder. "You know, you seem to enjoy talking about Patricia almost as much as Patricia does."

She couldn't help but smile. "Aren't you in love with her?"

"Do I *look* like a man who's in love with Patricia?"

He looked *exactly* like the man who had been in love with Patricia for years...so why wasn't he? She had seen the jolt in his expression when he'd first seen her on the television set in her father's living room. But now it seemed his visceral attraction to the woman had turned to a visceral repulsion.

At the present, unbelievably, it seemed he only had eyes for her. "You look perfectly silly in that big orange life preserver over your cast," she noted, tugging her hungry gaze away from his lips.

"And you look perfectly adorable." What seemed strange to her was that he sounded as if he meant it.

"Don't be ridiculous."

His eyebrows shot up with interest. "Hasn't anyone ever told you that before?"

"No! I mean, yes—of course." She huffed in frustration, mired in her own sense of realism. "Well, my father."

"No man's ever given you compliments like that before?"

She crossed her arms. "No, and what's more, I don't want them. Mainly I feel valued when someone compliments my integrity, or my abilities."

He rolled his eyes.

"It's true."

"It sounds like you've been hanging around the wrong men."

She let out a hoot—*he* was the principal man she'd been hanging around all this time. "You could be right."

He grinned again. "It's good to see you laugh, even if I'm not quite certain what you're laughing at."

Should she tell him that he'd unknowingly insulted himself? She considered it, then found that the thought had flown completely out of her mind, replaced by the undeniable anticipation of their promised kiss when Allan leaned closer to her.

"You are beautiful, you know."

She wasn't. But with the sun glinting off Allan's brown hair like a halo, he seemed so angelic that she allowed herself to accept the falsehood. In fact, she reveled in it. For just this one last time, she would kiss him and enjoy it, and then forever after try like the dickens to forget it ever happened.

In fact she was so stoically resolved now, she didn't even wait for him to kiss her. Leaning carefully toward him, she placed her arms on his shoulders and planted her lips on his. She had thought taking the initiative would sap some of the surprise out of the sensation of his lips against hers. It didn't. It had apparently caught Allan by surprise, though—and not in a good way from her point of view. He pulled her to him, nearly squeezing the air out of her, and deepened the kiss more than he might have just under his own steam.

In the moments that followed, she felt as if her good sense had blacked out as completely as Allan's memory. The sounds of gentle waves lapping against the rowboat, the gentle rolling motion and the playful machinations of Allan's tongue with hers all seemed bundled in one sensual package, special to this moment, this time and place. Never to be repeated, she kept telling herself.

This was it.

She savored his lips like a dieter tasting that last piece of chocolate cake.

Then, after long delectable moments of touching and tasting, the kiss was over. When Allan pulled away from her, she felt a blush heat her cheeks, and expected to find him gloating over her surprise attack on his lips. Instead, when she looked into his eyes, they were shining, not with mockery, but with an unquenched desire that she felt down to the depths of her soul, right alongside a quivering vulnerability that made her very, very nervous.

She remembered wishing once, back in the hospital, for Allan to be nice. Now she realized that old adage "Be careful what you wish for" bore a load of truth. Allan might be nice now—but he was even more dangerous nice than mean. Mean, she understood him, trusted him to be brutally honest with her. But how could she trust this Allan, with his flirtatious remarks and passionate kisses? How long could he go on before he reverted to his old self and realized that he had already decided he didn't love her? How long until he snapped out of it and realized that Patricia really was the woman for him?

Dangerous. She needed to get back to New York as soon as possible, back to work. There she would be able to shield herself from the temptation to flirt with Allan by throwing herself into day-to-day things, and finding a new job, and maybe a new apartment. One that would be better for a baby.

She scooted as far away from Allan as was physically possible, which in actuality was a paltry centimeter or two. "There," she said. "Are you satisfied?"

The words had a hollow, mocking ring to them that was reflected in his killer grin. He looked about as satisfied as a mosquito on a department store mannequin. "I hope that was a joke," he said.

She cleared her throat. "I believe we had a bargain."

He continued to look at her, as if he didn't quite get her meaning.

"Shouldn't you be getting back to the other end of the boat?" she prompted him.

"We should *both* be getting to the other side of the lake," he said. "And for that, I can help you."

"You?" she asked, nodding toward his sling.

"I can manage with my good arm." To demonstrate, he took a steady swipe at the water with one wooden oar, balancing it lightly against his knee. "See? One armed."

She pursed her lips. "You might have tried that little experiment before."

"But then I wouldn't have been able to enjoy the view."

"You can see fine from where I'm sitting."

"But from where I was sitting before, the view was much nicer, because I could watch you."

Dangerous, dangerous.

Jane hid her blush by concentrating on dipping her oar into the water. Even with one arm out of commission, Allan was a better rower than she was, and their progress across the lake increased exponentially. Unfortunately, their proximity on the little bench did not go unnoticed by the others as they approached the small landing on the opposite shore. Jane's father stood looking well pleased, his arms crossed in satisfaction.

Patricia, however, was another story.

ALLAN BIT BACK a laugh at the comical expression on Patricia's face as they approached the landing. She didn't even bother to hide the pout on her lips.

"My, my," Patricia noted as the boat made its first bump against the dock. "That certainly looks cozy."

"It is," Allan said. "It's also faster than having Jane row alone."

He looked over and thought he could detect the faintest hint of disappointment on Jane's face. Did she want them all to know that they had stopped to kiss halfway across the lake? He assumed that was pretty obvious, anyway, but he never would have thought that Jane—shy, practical Jane—would want the others to know.

Even if Patricia didn't know, she was as mad as a wet bee anyway. "You two certainly took your own sweet time. Will has half the food cooked, and I've practically been eaten alive by all these pesky bugs."

As if on cue, she slapped at an invisible flying critter that had landed on her leg. Even a woman as poised as Patricia couldn't look anything more than silly doing battle with a bug. And on closer inspection, she *did* appear to have been attacked by a swarm of something. Her skin had several bumps on it, and her arms were red from itching.

"Oh, this is just terrible!" she said. "I know these little bumps will show on camera."

"Don't scratch," Will told her.

Patricia just barely reined in a tart response. "That's easy for you to say. I haven't seen one measly little insect land on you."

Allan and Jane got out of their rowboat on the dock and pulled it by a rope far up onto the sandbank. Will looked at Allan and winked. So far, their plan had been successful. He'd had his first meaningful moments alone with Jane since Patricia had arrived.

"I've got a fire going," Will announced. "Come pick yourself out a wienie, if you want one."

"Hot dogs!" Patricia scoffed. "We did a story on them once on a health spot on the morning show. Wieners are just loaded with preservatives."

Allan grinned. "I know."

Both Jane and Patricia shook their heads. No doubt Jane wanted to tell him that he wasn't supposed to like hot dogs, either.

"I brought some chicken salad, if you'd prefer that," Jane suggested.

But his hand was already in the little plastic container, pulling out a frank. He might have hit that phone pole a finicky sourpuss, but he had awakened with the appetite of a ten-year-old. "Nonsense. A mustardy hot dog sounds great to me."

Jane turned to Patricia. "You're welcome to the chicken salad, too, Patricia," she offered, as generously as she could.

Patricia gave her a look of pure disdain, which sent an answering wave of anger through Allan. Especially when the blonde flounced over to his side and announced, "I always did like hot dogs, preservatives or no preservatives. Allan hates people who are too rigid, you know."

He supposed that was some sort of swipe at Jane; rather ineffectual, he thought. Patricia's razor-sharp competitiveness apparently grew more hysterical in the great outdoors. She was now trying to best Jane on the subject of wienies.

Lunch was hardly the peaceful affair the beautiful country setting would have called for. Patricia insisted on regaling everyone with ideas for "America Alive!" and Will took every opportunity to point out the peculiar fact that the mosquitoes and gnats were attracted only to Patricia.

The more they talked about this phenomenon, the more irritated Patricia became.

Will, being a true gentleman of the old-fashioned variety, opined that insects were naturally drawn to things that were sweet and beautiful. But Allan decided the attraction was actually the sickly-sweet scent she drenched herself in several times a day. "Unforgettable" seemed to beckon flying insects more effectively than men.

Which was another reason to stay away from her, Allan noted as he downed his third hot dog. He considered going for a fourth, just to get away from Patricia, but he knew she'd manage to slither back to him again. And besides, every time he took another hot dog, Jane looked at him in amazement, as if he had somehow lost his mind.

Which, of course, he had. He remembered her telling him something about his being health conscious. Funny, he didn't seem to have very many healthy cravings. His strongest desire was for Jane herself, and how healthy was that? She apparently wanted nothing to do with him, no matter how much she might be attracted to him.

And he did catch her tossing him little sidelong glances as she dutifully ate her lonely chicken salad. Why did she insist that he give Patricia a chance when he so obviously preferred her? It was almost as if she refused to believe that a man could really find her desirable, an idea he found ludicrous. Apparently, no man had yet lavished on her the affection she deserved.

"Should have brought ice cream," Will said.

Patricia nearly had a conniption at the very idea. "Ice cream! Are you serious? That stuff is just *loaded* with calories!"

Happily, they were saved from an in-depth discussion of this wearisome topic by an approaching boat. Will got up and walked to the little dock, where he was soon joined by the three others. The interest they all showed in the new arrival made them seem as desperate for news of the outside world as the cast of "Gilligan's Island."

"Oh, no!" Jane cried out when the man was near enough for her to recognize him.

Allan still didn't have the faintest idea who it was. All he saw was a man, blond and handsomely decked out in a red shirt and stiff blue jeans, speeding toward them in a motorboat, his reflective sunglasses giving him the appearance of a yuppie bug. Idly, Allan wondered whether he had been drawn here by Patricia's sweet perfume, too.

"Oh, no," Patricia muttered.

Jane ran out to meet the boat, giving Allan his first hint of uncertainty. Despite everyone's "Oh, no's," Jane seemed *awfully* eager to reach this fellow, whoever he was. He shot an inquiring glance Will's way, but the older man merely sent him a droopy shrug.

"Grady!" Jane cried. "What are you doing here?"

Allan's ears perked up. Grady? Grady Grimly? In all his days of hearing about the man, he had never expected him to look like this. Over the phone, and from hearsay, he would have guessed that Grady would be paunchy and jaundiced-looking from years of dividing his time between a psychiatrist's couch and the cavernous beehive that was Wall Street. This man resembled a shorter, less smarmy John Tesh.

Though when Grady took off his glasses, Allan noted happily that the man wasn't quite as handsome as he'd thought at first. He had a desperate, owl-eyed appearance. And his mouth, even as he greeted Jane and accepted her hand up to the dock, was locked in a line of uncertainty that looked as if it might be permanent.

Grady flicked an uncertain gaze at Patricia and Allan, nodding curtly. "Allan told me."

Jane frowned. "Told you what?"

"That Patricia was staying here."

Good, Allan thought. Grady might take Patricia off their hands.

Then he frowned. Hadn't Jane said that Grady was in love with *her?*

Allan immediately moved in closer. "What does Patricia have to do with anything?" he asked.

"Yes," Patricia chimed in.

Grady looked at all of them with the same perplexed set to his mouth. "With Patricia here, you don't need Jane, do you?"

Patricia was pleased no end by this statement. "That's just what I've been trying to tell everyone all along!"

"Jane needs to come back to New York," Grady announced. "I've brought my car for her."

Allan sputtered at the man's high-handedness. "You can't just take Jane away. This is her home, you know."

Grady looked at Jane—a little too soulfully for Allan's taste. "Don't you want to come back with me?"

"Now?" she asked, her voice barely a squeak.

"Of course now."

Jane shook her head. "Oh, Grady, you shouldn't have come out all this way. What were you thinking of?"

"You."

She crossed her arms. "Well, it so happens that I *am* going back to New York," she said, shooting a glance toward Allan.

"What?" Will and Allan exclaimed simultaneously.

She turned to them. "It's true. I made up my mind this morning."

Grady smiled. "Good, then you can come back with me right now."

She rolled her eyes as he took her arm. "Grady, no," she said, digging in her heels.

"What's the matter?" he asked impatiently. "You don't want to stay out here, do you?"

"I'm having lunch," she said, pointing to her discarded chicken salad sandwich several yards away.

"I'll buy you lunch," he replied. "A real one. We'll stop by the Russian Tea Room on our way into town."

"Grady—"

"Besides," he said, cutting her off as he screwed up his face distastefully, "you don't want to stay out here. I'm sure it can't be healthy. What's that smell?"

His wrinkled nose expression landed squarely on Patricia, who squirmed uncomfortably.

"That's not a *smell*," she corrected him, "it's a very expensive fragrance that came all the way from Paris."

He looked at her face, with its red bumps. "Well, you should rinse it off," he said bluntly. "I think it's giving you a rash."

Patricia quaked with rage. "That's not a rash. Those are insect bites!"

All the while, Grady tugged Jane toward his motorboat, causing Allan to bridle indignantly. Who did he think he was, manipulating Jane this way?

Before Grady could budge her another inch, Allan reached out and took her other arm, anchoring her. Grady looked at him and frowned.

"Now you stay out of this, Allan," he warned. "You might be her boss, but I'm the one who loves her."

Jane sputtered unhappily, as did her father. "See here!" Will cried, clamping a steadying hand onto Jane's shoulder. "My daughter's not going anywhere with you, young man."

Grady remained focused on Jane. "Are you coming or not?" He gave her arm another yank—which must have been powerful, because it caused the cluster around Jane to take another collective step toward the edge of the dock.

"Grady!" she cried. "Will you stop?"

Her resistance, apparently, just made Grady all that more determined. And then Patricia joined his team, apparently forgetting his rash dig in favor of his taking Jane away.

"Of course she wants to go back to New York," Patricia said, pulling on Grady's shoulder. "And Grady's BMW is so-o-o much more comfortable than the nasty old train."

Her words began an all-out tug-of-war over Jane, which lasted until the moment Grady's heel hit the edge of the dock. He toppled over and hit the water with a solid splash, which was followed by two more splashes as, one by one, Patricia and Jane followed him into the water.

Allan hadn't expected to fall, but his bum arm had him off balance. He teetered precariously for a long moment before finally dropping off the edge. Oh, well, he thought philosophically, at least he'd have sogginess in common with Jane.

But as he plunged into the cool water, besides a jarring of his arm, he felt a tug of memory. Something someone had said recently. Jane, he thought. When was it?

Oh, yes, he thought, just beginning to panic. Back on the boat, when she'd been telling him to sit down... He remembered her words quite clearly now, and they repeated mockingly in his head.

"Allan, you can't swim!"

Chapter Six

"Allan, you can't swim!"

Jane couldn't keep the hysteria out of her voice as she trod water frantically, waiting to see his head break the surface.

She saw Patricia, soaking wet, hauling herself up on the dock, aided by Will. Grady had just made it to the water's edge. But Allan...

Just then, she caught sight of his head. Harking all the way back to the days of junior lifesaving lessons, Jane called out, "Try to keep your head up, Allan—I'll be right there!" She swam like crazy, and even though there was only a short distance between them, her nervousness made her feel as if she had more pressure on her than Janet Evans at the Olympic Games. By the time she reached Allan and braced an arm around his neck, as she had seen rescuers do on television, she felt as if her lungs might explode.

"Keep breathing, Allan," she instructed, "we're gonna make it."

"Jane..." His words were lost at sea when she accidentally dunked his head—and hers—underwater.

"Don't talk," she said, her voice a hoarse, breathless

burble. She had swallowed half a lake of water, and her nerves were still in high gear. "Just float. Float, Allan."

Something hit her on the side of the head. She looked to her side and saw a buoy. "Grab onto that if you're so determined to float, Janie."

She stopped, looking at her father. Patricia and Grady had congregated around him and they were all staring down at her with perplexed expressions. Then, in the ensuing silence, she noticed that Allan was standing in the water, staring at her, too.

Standing.

Oh, dear.

She dipped her toe down and felt it barely hit the sandy bottom of the lake. She had been so keyed up she hadn't noticed that Allan wasn't drowning at all. Embarrassed by her blunder, she wordlessly grabbed the ring and began to kick. She didn't even make a peep when Allan grabbed on and started tugging her toward the dock. The lifesaver being rescued, she moaned to herself.

"It's the thought that counts," Allan whispered appreciatively in her ear.

The feel of his breath caused a sensual shiver to jump across her spine, and God help her, she turned to look into his eyes. Big mistake. The desire his sexy grin caused to leap to life in her would take eight lakes' worth of cold water to douse.

She really was taking leave of her senses, she decided.

She needed to get out of here. Back to Manhattan.

She forced her gaze away from Allan, and it landed, appropriately enough, on Grady, who was still standing impatiently on the dock next to her father, checking his watch. He might have been waiting for his chauffeur on the corner of Fifth Avenue, so oblivious did he seem to the fact that a small stream from his sopping-wet jeans was trickling away from his loafers.

Next to him, Patricia was drenched through, her little checkered dress sticking to her like a second, very revealing skin. She twitched, shaking out one limb at a time like a cat that had just been rescued from a fall into a bathtub. "What were you trying to do, drown us all?" Patricia said to Grady.

Grady pointed to his dripping shirt, all innocence. "Me?" he asked. "*You* were the one who pushed everyone in."

"I did no such thing!"

"In fact, I think you did it on purpose, because I made some innocent little comment about your bug bites."

"Innocent!" Patricia huffed. "You said I had a rash—which was pure viciousness. I've never been prone to skin blemishes! You've never liked me. And now everyone is against me—just because I made one measly mistake!"

Grady as well as Will appeared completely nonplussed by her tirade. Patricia stood in front of them looking more and more miserable, on the verge of tears, until she saw Allan coming out of the water. Immediately, she ran to his side.

"Oh, Allan, thank God you're all right!" she cried, launching herself at him. The poor woman looked so pathetic that even Jane had to feel pity for her—until she saw Patricia's cool stare, focused right on her. That glare didn't disguise any of Patricia's unhappiness, or the malice she'd been holding in check these past few days.

Oh, yes, Jane thought. She needed to get out of there. Pronto.

"Grady," Jane asked meekly as her father gave her a lift back onto the dock, "are you still going back to New York today?"

"HONESTLY, JANE," Grady said in a tone that was half lecture, half whine, "I don't know what's gotten into you."

He shot her a sideways glance as they sped onto the highway. Grady's blond hair was still wet and plastered to his head, making him look as if he had Brylcream in it. Which, combined with the Ward Cleaver tone he was taking with her, was the perfect effect.

"I told you marrying Allan was a bad idea," he reminded her. "I said, 'He's still in love with Patricia. He's on the rebound. It'll never work.'"

"You were right, Grady," she admitted.

But he didn't seem interested in her agreement. "Not to mention, he's got all those investments in developing countries. Very risky. You wouldn't see me doing that."

"You're right."

He looked at her pleadingly. "If you want to marry somebody, why don't you marry me? Isn't it obvious that I'm the better bet?"

"I wasn't gambling, Grady," she replied. Then, ducking her head, she admitted, "I thought...well, I was foolishly following the dictates of my heart."

Also, she had thought she was going to marry the father of her child, however impractical and old-fashioned that might seem nowadays.

"Bad, bad, bad idea," Grady mumbled, shaking his head. "Haven't I told you a million times? Following your heart, gut reactions, spur-of-the-moment impulses—that's women's magazine stuff. You've got to forget about all that and plan things out carefully.''

"Is this what your psychiatrist tells you?" she asked in amazement.

"Of course not. If you take all your advice from one source it's like mental totalitarianism. My philosophy is and always has been a healthy combination of Dr. Winkel, *GQ*, and *Modern Money* magazine."

Jane gave his previous words some thought and sighed. "You're right," she repeated. He *was* right. She had known marrying Allan was risky, and sure enough, it had all blown up in her face.

"Then why don't you marry me?" he asked. "I'm just the ticket for all your marital needs. Good-looking, rich, stable."

She looked at him and laughed. "You've been going to a psychiatrist every Thursday afternoon since you were twenty-two."

He nodded vigorously. "Twelve years and counting with Dr. Winkel. How much more stable can you get? I tell you, Jane, it's like one-stop husband shopping. I've got everything you could possibly want."

She took a deep breath. Everything except for the fact that she wasn't in love with him. Of course, Grady would just dismiss that as more "women's magazine stuff." And maybe it was. She was certainly in a fix. But she just couldn't jump into Grady's arms at the first roadblock. That would be no better than what Allan had done to her.

"What I don't understand is why you could possibly want me, Grady."

"What are you talking about? You're beautiful, incredibly efficient and you've got a great head for business."

Funny, Allan had told her the exact same thing about four weeks ago. But when Allan had said the words, they had sounded like a romantic pronouncement. So why, coming from Grady's lips, did the same description of her seem vaguely insulting?

She sent him an even stare. "I'm not as pretty as other women I've seen you with, and you would shudder to know that I've only had one year when I was able to save ten percent of my salary."

He *did* shudder, visibly, and two worry lines appeared at the bridge of his nose. "Really?"

"It's true. I love to spend money."

He considered this disturbing fact for at least fifteen miles. The next time he opened his mouth, in fact, Jane half expected a retraction of his previous proposals. Instead, he swallowed and stuttered bravely, "It—it's okay." That said, he tossed his head in a devil-may-care manner. "Yes, I can handle that."

"Handle what?"

"Your spending," he explained. "The way I figure it, you've never been filthy rich before. Naturally you like to spend money. I think this trip to Vermont has been very beneficial. Aside from rescuing you from Allan's clutches, I've come to understand the distressed circumstances of your upbringing."

She laughed, though there was a bit of scorched pride in it. "My father's dairy was quite successful. Not everyone could be born on Park Avenue, you know."

"All right, but I'll certainly make allowances if you're a bit of a shopaholic in the beginning."

"That's big of you."

He shrugged. "Oh, you'll learn. Once you've gone

through your first million, it's all fairly boring. The best thing about money is watching it pile up. And married to me, you'll have a lot of piles to watch."

She shook her head. After five years on Wall Street, she could never understand how someone could approach life so single-mindedly obsessed with one thing, even if it was a detail as significant as money.

"You're hopeless, Grady," she said finally, throwing up her hands.

He lifted a finger from the leather-lined steering wheel and waggled it in her direction. "Not hopeless. *Hopeful.* I think you might still change your mind."

"I wouldn't bank on it." She didn't want to lie to him. Not that the truth had ever discouraged him before.

"Well...at least we've got you off your Allan jag." In the silence that followed, another set of worry lines appeared in his forehead. "Haven't we?"

"We have," she lied emphatically.

He nodded, satisfied with that tiny step at least. "Good. Mind if we swing by the office?"

So much for romance, as Grady defined it.

But then, why not pop by the office? Back to Manhattan, back to work. With Junior on the way, she needed to get serious about planning her future. "Swing away, Grady."

Unfortunately, back at Steele and Grimly, she realized that her Allan jag, as Grady so aptly termed it, was still very much jagging her concentration. He was impossible to forget. Everywhere she turned, she would see his nameplate, or his signature, or mail addressed to him. And every time she saw that name, she couldn't help thinking how close she had come to being Mrs. Allan Steele.

After an hour, when she discovered herself doodling

the initials A.S. all over a spreadsheet, like a besotted junior high girl, she knew she had to get out of there.

Being back at her apartment, however, didn't do her that much good. The first thing she did was pack away her wedding dress in its original box and stuff it in the closet. But the box was so big, and her matchbox closet was so small, that the wedding dress kept popping back out again like a poltergeist. She would return it first thing Saturday. Hopefully she could still get her money back. With a baby on the way, she needed to start being more frugal...and what better place to start?

Yet once she had unpacked she found herself at loose ends once again. Tired from the day's ordeal, she sank down on her bed and closed her eyes. And then she remembered.

This was the bed where she and Allan had made love.

Her eyes popped open and she trudged to her kitchenette to make herself some hot cocoa. She needed something soothing to get her head back on straight, to get back on track again. What she desperately needed was to get back to work, back to the routine. Back in the old groove.

With that resolve firmly fixed in her mind, the next day she did something that she had only done twice before in all her years with Steele and Grimly. She called in sick.

WHERE THE HECK was Jane?

She was supposed to be his loyal assistant, but now, when he needed her most, she was gone. In Vermont, she had been breathing down his neck with work every waking minute. Now, however, he hadn't seen her all day—and the day before she had called in sick.

Allan felt at sea without her. Even his apartment was

a puzzle. Jane had written his address down, so he knew—on paper at least—that he resided there. But in reality, it didn't look like anyone really *lived* there. There were no family pictures to give him a clue to his identity, no pictures on the walls to even give him a clue as to his tastes. The magazines he'd found lying about were all financial in nature, and there simply were no books. The furniture was all sturdy oak, except for a hunter green couch that sat in front of an entertainment center that seemed to rise up out of nowhere, black and imposing.

It was all so empty—just like that niggling emptiness he felt inside himself sometimes. The place needed stuff on the walls, more fabrics to break the monotony of wood and white walls, it needed a kitten running around scratching things up. It needed some visible sign of life, some evidence of caring. Just as he needed Jane.

But now he was at work, and instead of Jane he was surrounded by a small legion of other employees whose purpose he couldn't remember, who looked at him with confusion when he asked where the paper clips were, and the water cooler.

"Doesn't Jane know?" they would invariably ask. Or, in the case of the water cooler, one smart aleck replied, "Do you mean you've never had a glass of water since founding this business, Mr. Steele?"

And when Allan had snickered at the lame joke, the poor young man who had made the remark recoiled from him as if he expected to be fired. As if he'd never heard Allan Steele laugh at a joke before.

Come to think of it, that was the same reaction he'd gotten from Jane when he'd tried to flirt with her in the hospital.

Okay, so maybe the old Allan didn't flirt and didn't

laugh. He probably didn't sit around the office making ice cream in the employee kitchen, either. That had raised a few eyebrows. Well, things had changed. The only carryover he actually was interested in keeping from his old life was Jane, and she was nowhere to be found.

Until, unexpectedly, she came swinging into the kitchen, clutching her briefcase, and nearly knocked the blueberry fudge ripple right out of his hand. She turned the corner, ran smack into his chest, looked up and sucked in a breath of surprise.

God, she was gorgeous. In the two days since he'd last seen her, he had thought perhaps his memory was exaggerating the effect those green eyes had on him, but it hadn't been.

"What are you doing here?" she asked a little breathlessly.

That was how he felt. Breathless. Just looking at her made his heart thump a million times a minute, making it hard to take in enough air. Lacking lung power, he settled for extending a spoonful of ice cream with his good arm. "Have some?" he managed to say.

She glanced warily from the spoon to the corner of the kitchen where her father's old wooden ice cream maker stood looking about as out of place as Zelda the cow herself might have. "Oh, no," she moaned.

He smiled, tweaking her red lips with the ice cream. Jane was wearing makeup, he noted for the first time. "C'mon," he coaxed, "it's blueberry."

"Allan, do you have any idea how much worked piled up while we were away?"

"Do *you* have any idea how hard it is to get fresh blueberries this time of year? I had to go all the way to

Balducci's—I think they were flown in from Madagascar or Outer Mongolia or somewhere.''

She lifted her briefcase, shielding herself with it as if it were an armor breastplate, and tapped her fingers impatiently against the thick shiny leather. ''I have at least a hundred flags for your attention on the monthly investor reports, and Clyde Siming—'' Her voice stopped abruptly as she focused on his chest. ''Allan, you're wearing a Snoopy tie.''

''Isn't it cute? Picked it up at Macy's this morning.''

Her frown grew deeper. ''Macy's? You mean you came into work late?''

''Hey, I'm the boss.''

''Yes,'' she agreed with growing desperation, ''and you're also one of the most formidable figures in the New York financial world, and you're wearing a tie with a dog and a little yellow bird on it!''

''All right, all right, calm down,'' he said, dropping the spoon. ''For your information, I *saw* those reports and looked over them. Most of them.''

She nodded.

He gazed at her more closely. She was wearing a conservative blue suit, very tailored, with matching blue pumps that made her legs look dynamite. ''Where have you been?'' he asked.

She shifted her weight a few times. ''Around.''

''Are you feeling all right?''

''Yes, of course.'' She stared at him blankly.

''You called in sick yesterday.'' She didn't look sick. Just the opposite. Her hair was shiny clean and hanging neatly around her chin, and her cheeks bloomed with health.

''Oh, that. Well…I must have picked up a bug back

home, I guess," she said. She looked down at his sling. "Is your arm okay?"

"McGillicutty said I'd be good as new—as long as I didn't try to become the first person to swim one-armed around New York harbor."

She wasn't laughing at that, either. "Where's Patricia?"

"Probably off getting a facial. Or her hair fixed. Did she tell you she uses the same hairdresser as Katie Couric?"

Jane smiled faintly. "A few dozen times."

"He uses a lighter shade of dye on Patricia, though. 'Ashened Wheat,' I think it's called. I heard all about it on the way back from your father's."

She shifted nervously. "I should be getting back to my desk...."

Allan didn't want her to go just yet. "Do you always look like this at work?"

"Look how?" she asked, staring up at him with those green eyes.

He grinned. "Like a million bucks."

Two spots of red bloomed in her cheeks. Then they abruptly faded at the sound of someone clearing his throat behind her.

She twirled, and Allan looked up to see Grady standing there, glancing anxiously between them.

"You two seem to be having fun," Grady said humorlessly. He crossed his arms, rocked on his heels and looked down at the spoonful of melting ice cream in Allan's hand. "Ice cream?"

"I made it myself," Allan bragged. "Blueberry chocolate ripple."

Jane looked a little like a kid who had been caught

chewing gum in class. "He had to go all the way to Balducci's."

"Well isn't that great," Grady said, turning sharp eyes on Allan. "Who do you think you are, Ben and Jerry?"

Allan grinned. "Just imagine, Grady, if the business ever goes under, we'll be all set to open the Wall Street Ice Cream Emporium."

At the incredulous look on Grady's face, Jane made her excuses and slipped away. Grady watched her go and turned on Allan. He, too, noted the Snoopy tie and rolled his eyes impatiently. In a low voice, he said, "Look, Jane has told me that you're not feeling quite...shall we say, yourself. But are you sure you should even be here?"

"What do you mean?"

"Well, for one thing, while you're in the kitchen playing Betty Crocker, the price of oil is dropping like a lead balloon."

He didn't see that as any reason to go into a dither. "Okay, so it's dropping."

His lackadaisical tone nearly caused Grady to go into a swivet. "We have clients to think of, Allan. We're supposed to be making money."

Allan patted his nervous partner on the back. "Quit worrying."

That only agitated him more. "You're the one who should be worried," Grady admonished. "Ever since you've become obsessed over Patricia, Jane's been the one who's kept your side going. And now she's going on job interviews."

Allan froze. "Did Jane tell you that?"

Grady screwed up his lips and answered sagely, "She didn't have to. I know Jane, and what's more, I know the signs. Blue suit. Snappy briefcase. Long disappearing acts in the middle of the day.'' Finally, seeing the anxious look on Allan's face, Grady smiled. ''Oh, sure, it's clear she's had it up to here working for you, Allan. And if you don't watch out, I just might try to woo her over to my side.''

That's what he was afraid of, Allan thought as he watched Grady turn and make his way down the hall, whistling a jaunty version of ''Pennies from Heaven.'' He wasn't sure how expert Grady was at wooing, but he feared that the man was pestering Jane for more than her business acumen.

As soon as Grady rounded the corner, Allan dashed after Jane, who was fussing busily around her cubicle.

''So...how did it go?''

She whirled in surprise. ''How did what go?''

''The interview.'' When her eyes registered faint astonishment, he leaned casually against the wall and in his best Grady imitation, said, ''Oh, sure. I know what's going on. Blue suit, snappy briefcase...''

''You've been talking to your partner.''

He smiled. ''That, too. Honestly, I don't understand. Have I done anything to offend you?''

She hesitated. ''N-no...''

''Then why would you want to leave?'' He peeked around the corner to make sure no one was listening, then added, ''From what I've heard about the old me, I think I can safely say that things are just now beginning to get a little fun around here.''

''*Fun* isn't exactly what I was looking for in a job, Allan. Now about Mr. Simington. He's going to be in town next week, and it's very important that we—''

''I think it's very important that you have dinner with me tonight.''

"You already have dinner plans."

He drew back. "I do?"

She nodded. "Patricia just called to tell you so. I marked it on your desk calendar."

Was he kidding himself, or did her Miss Efficiency routine seem to be covering something else? "Well, why don't we cancel on her?"

"Can't," Jane answered briskly. "She's taping right now. Remember? Poor schmucky Americans wouldn't know what they were up to without Patricia pointing it out to them." She flicked a file drawer closed and sauntered right past him, into his office.

Allan followed. "There has to be some way to make contact with the news media. Can't we E-mail her or something?"

She placed a file folder on his desk. "Allan, I can't go out to dinner with you."

"Why not?"

"Because we work together."

"So did Clark Kent and Lois Lane."

"Yes," she said reasonably, "but they were cartoons."

He thought for a moment. "Is this why you're changing jobs?"

"Absolutely not. Look, Allan, you might not see the danger in the situation, but believe me, I do."

"I take it you're speaking from bad past experience."

She shot him a level stare.

He shrugged his shoulders miserably. The poor girl probably just wanted to get away from Grady pestering her at work all day, and who could blame her? But why did *he* have to pay for Grady's sins? "Then it's hopeless. You won't go out with me now, and once you find a new job, you probably won't answer my phone calls."

"I think that's probably for the best, don't you?" she asked. "You really should spend more time with Patricia."

Why was she always throwing him together with Patricia? It was like torture! "But—"

She turned, her ears perking up like a spaniel's at the inaudible tone of a dog whistle. "That's my phone. It could be Clyde. What should I tell him?"

Allan looked blankly at her.

She thought for a moment, then said, "I'll tell him that we're concerned but not alarmed about oil."

"Speak for yourself," Allan quipped. And before she could disappear into the hallway, he heard her mutter, "Comedian!" and smiled to himself.

Oh, he was getting to her all right. Slowly but surely he was making progress.

Like a turtle climbing Pike's Peak.

"STEELE AND GRIMLY, Jane Fielding speaking."

There was a strange smugness in the pause that followed that let Jane know in advance exactly whom she was dealing with. It had to be Patricia.

"Da-a-a-arling," Patricia purred, as if they were long-lost buddies. "How *are* you doing?"

Jane gritted her teeth. "Fine."

"Terrif. Well, I suppose your boss is hard at work."

Patricia still didn't get the fact that her fiancé wasn't quite the man he used to be. Jane smiled. "I imagine he's either making ice cream or playing darts in the break room."

"Oh." Patricia took this in, as well as Jane's apparent unwillingness to go fetch him for her, and finally answered, "Well, as long as he's there. We have a dinner date tonight, naturally—"

Patricia had cadged a meal off Allan every night since they returned from Vermont, with Jane's sinister aid.

"But I thought I might pop by beforehand...."

Jane suddenly lost the thread of conversation and was sent cross-eyed by a close-up of an ice cream cone in her face. As always, Allan's arm was attached to it. He beamed a grin at her meant to telegraph that he was the most charming thing on earth—which he actually was, darn it.

She'd thought that once they both returned to New York, things might change. That he might get a little of his old sourness back, which would make it easier for her to harden her heart against him. No such luck. Instead, he was running around the office in cartoon ties, and she was more attracted to him than ever.

Which meant that she needed to redouble her efforts to get away from him. Unfortunately, it wasn't going to be so easy to find another job. The job market was tight, and besides, she didn't have the nerve to lie about her pregnancy. And the minute a personnel person heard that she was expecting, he or she would suddenly avoid Jane's eyes and look down at her résumé as if it had Adolf Hitler typed across the top of it.

So much for the "family friendly" cant these companies spouted. She would probably be making dinner dates for Patricia and Allan right up to the moment her water broke.

An idea occurred to her. She smiled and interrupted Patricia, who was still chattering on the other end of the line. "Why, you're in luck! Allan's right here."

At Allan's curious gaze, she mouthed Patricia's name, which sent him into a conniption of hand signals telling her he wasn't available to take the call.

"Just a minute, I'll put him on."

Allan was just attempting to sneak away when Jane snatched the cone from his hand and handed the receiver to him. She derived real pleasure watching him lean against her desk in a sulk and mumble into the receiver, "Hi, Patricia."

Jane took a lick of ice cream, something she kept trying to avoid. But as a blend of vanilla and mint burst upon her tastebuds, she suddenly wondered why. This was delicious! The mint was so fresh she could see the green from chopped up bits of leaves. Allan was definitely going for the ultra-homemade effect with this one. Or maybe that was simply the best he could do in the office kitchen. She licked happily at the cone as she eavesdropped on his conversation with Patricia. Not that there was much to hear.

"Really?" Allan looked at Jane and rolled his eyes. "Oh...well... All right..." Only half listening to Patricia, he mouthed the word "mint" to Jane. She nodded, and gave him a thumbs up signal.

He smiled. Then he cocked his head against the receiver. "Sorry, I wasn't lis—I mean, I'm a little preoccupied here, naturally. Uh-huh. We've just been swamped with work. Did you hear about the price of oil?" He frowned at something Patricia was saying. "Darts? I don't know what you mean."

Jane laughed.

"Well, all right. I'll see you soon, then."

He hung up the phone and hopped off the desk. "She's on her way over," he said, his tone verging on desperation. "I've got to make a quick escape."

"But, Allan, you just said you'd be here."

He turned on her. "This is all your fault," he accused. "You're the one who thinks I should keep seeing her."

"It would be terrible if you dumped her for no reason, Allan."

"No reason?" he asked incredulously. "She left me at the altar and ran off with a married man!"

It was nice to see him get a taste of his own medicine, even if he didn't realize it. Jane lifted her shoulders. "She apologized, didn't she?"

He looked at her skeptically. "Whose side are you on?"

Jane stood. "No one's. I'm just an innocent bystander."

His eyes narrowed. "Not so innocent, I'll bet."

She felt a fluttery feeling inside at the slightly gravelly quality of his voice. Did this new Allen really find her attractive, or was he just a hopeless flirt?

"I need to get some things copied," she told him, attempting to sashay past him.

He blocked her path. "Won't I ever get to talk to you alone, away from this place?"

Jane smiled crisply, and tried to ignore the quick frisson of desire that leaped through her when he touched her lightly on the arm. The man could make any square inch of skin seem like an erogenous zone. "Patricia's invited me to a party at her apartment next month. Well, actually, she said she was inviting a lot of her help, and that naturally I could come too if I wanted."

"Patricia, Patricia," he moaned with frustration. "Do you realize you always bring the subject around to her?"

"And do you realize that you always want to go running in the other direction when I mention her? That could get to be a bad habit. She's still your fiancée, Allan, for all intents and purposes.''

"God forbid!" he cried. "I only go out with her because you act as if I would be some kind of monster if I didn't. And you keep on answering the phone and making dinner dates with her."

"That's because you're never in your office to answer the phone yourself," she said. "And I simply don't want you to burn your bridges. Who knows? You might be back to your old self tomorrow, in which case you'll thank me for saving your relationship with Patricia."

Allan leaned back against her desk, sending her a mock scowl. "Thank you? In the case of Patricia, the only thing I'd thank you for is telling her I've moved to Tibet to become a monk!"

Jane laughed at the idea of either of the Allans doing such a thing. For that matter, so did Allan.

And then she looked over to see Grady standing in the doorway of her cubicle, looking anxiously from her face to her boss's. Since Allan's return from Vermont, Grady's expression had been ricocheting between smug self-assurance and withering anxiety and lack of confidence. While that was pretty much par for the course, Jane feared she was now at the core of Grady's worries, even though she had assured him many times that she was over Allan.

"Good to see you two having a nice time," he said petulantly.

Allan's smile didn't fade, but Jane could see a change in his demeanor. A gritty determination not to back down. "Anything we can help you with, Grimly?" he asked.

"Actually, I just came over to talk to Jane for a minute."

Grady appeared nonplussed that Allan wasn't going back to his office. Hadn't budged an inch, as a matter of fact.

Jane cleared her throat, beginning to feel a tad nervous at the conflict she was creating between the two men. "What is it, Grady?"

"Well, I…" He shot Allan a resentful look, then puffed up bravely. "If you must know, I came over to ask you if you would join me for dinner."

That said, he shot Allan a look that said *So there!*

Suddenly, Jane wished that Allan had left. She didn't want to make Grady think she was interested in him, but she didn't want to refuse the invitation in front of Allan.

Ducking her head, she said in a low voice, "I'm sorry, Grady, I've got plans."

At which point Allan sent Grady a look that also said *So there!*

Jane rolled her eyes. Honestly, these two might have met at Harvard Business School, but at the moment they were acting like two bullies in a schoolyard. She was about to tell them so, too, when she was distracted by a rustling noise outside her cubicle, then blinded by a startling vision in white.

When her poor pupils were able to focus again, she saw that it was Patricia, all decked out in a wedding dress, complete with train and veil and bouquet. It looked like something from the twenties.

Allan and Grady were also staring at Patricia in eye-popping surprise, and who could blame them?

"You like?" Patricia asked, striking several glamorous poses for Allan—vampy poses that contrasted completely with the demure dress she was sporting.

Allan swallowed. "Wh-what are you doing here?" he sputtered.

"I told you I was just a few blocks away!" Patricia said. "Weren't you listening?"

Obviously he hadn't been.

Patricia made a valiant attempt at shaking off her irritation. "Anyway," she said, smiling a little too stiffly, "this was the little surprise I was telling you about. Like it?"

Allan blinked as he looked over the mock-flapper dress. "Well, sure…"

"'America Alive!' is doing a feature on retro-weddings. You know, women copying their grandmother's old dresses and all that? It'll be perfect for a light, pre-June segment."

"Oh, sure," Allan agreed.

Patricia winked at him flirtatiously. "Give you any ideas, Allan?"

Jane's stomach began to churn. Maybe because, from her point of view, Allan was eyeing Patricia's statuesque figure a little too appreciatively. But who could blame him? She *was* beautiful, and certainly not shy when it came to letting the world know it.

When Allan failed to reply, Patricia sank back down to her off-camera stature, pouting slightly like an underappreciated goddess. "Well, I can see I've interrupted something."

"Yes, in fact—"

"No!" Jane cried, cutting off Allan's words. It was silly of her to sit around feeling jealous of Patricia, since she herself wanted nothing to do with Allan. In fact, this was all to the good. Allan *deserved* to be saddled with Patricia in her June bride outfit. And Jane deserved to get on with her own life—apart from Allan.

Jane turned to Patricia, smiling as genuinely as she could manage, and said, "As a matter of fact, I was just making arrangements to have dinner with Grady."

"Oh, you were?" Patricia beamed happily.

"You were?" Grady chimed in, surprised, but he also was wearing a smile.

The only one who *wasn't* smiling was Allan.

Chapter Seven

Rio's was one of the hottest new restaurants on the Upper West Side, and Jane could easily see why the place was so popular. The dining room was all done up in stucco painted in bright carnival colors, with a live band in the corner playing nonstop samba tunes that made even the most staid Manhattanites tap their feet and wiggle in their seats in muted imitation of hot-blooded Latins. And there were always a few couples vamping beneath the heavy iron chandelier over the dance floor, providing entertainment for the other patrons and obstacles for the busy waiters, who rushed around in black pants and crisp white shirts with ruffly sleeves.

It was all a little hokey, but Grady promised that the food was excellent. He also highly recommended a particularly potent-looking cocktail called an Anaconda. In fact, he was so eager to ply her with liquor that Jane feared he was actually trying to get her drunk. Thinking of the baby, she happily abstained from ordering anything stronger than iced tea, which was a good thing, since Grady was drinking enough for all three of them. He seemed determined that this would be their big night, an idea that made Jane more than a little nervous. Especially when he downed his third straight Anaconda with a single slug and a wink. He definitely imagined that the romantic pressure was on—and he was cracking beneath it.

Poor guy, Jane thought. Right now, in another of his hard-sell ploys to get her to marry him, he was going on about the joys of Westchester.

"I tell you, Jane, for what we're both paying in Manhattan now, we can have a place in Westchester that makes my penthouse look like a slum!"

Since Grady lived at one of the most exclusive addresses in town, she found his words a little hard to believe. And a little excessive. "For one thing," she told him, "I live in Brooklyn, and if I did move I'd just like a place big enough to house me and my wardrobe both."

He frowned at her through an Anaconda-induced fog. "I didn't know you were a clotheshorse."

"I'm not," she explained. "It's just the apartment I rent is very small."

"*Rent!*" he cried, so loudly that even some of the dancers looked over at their table in alarm. "Are you out of your mind? No, no, no! Shouldn't rent. Why, that's like throwing your money down through a subway grate!"

Taking his fountain pen from his jacket and using his napkin as a notepad, for the next ten minutes Grady calculated how much they would save by combining incomes and buying a big place in Westchester County.

Jane spent ten minutes wondering how many Anacondas a man could consume before he passed out. "Grady, surely my measly income couldn't make that much difference to you."

He looked up from his napkin, practically slack-jawed in amazement at her statement. "It's not just a matter of income, Jane," he said as if explaining this to a small child, "it's the write-offs and tax shelters. It's the efficiency of supporting a unit of two instead of an individual. Now consider this...."

Jane felt her eyes glazing over, and was rescued from a purely theoretical discussion of the value of marriage when their waiter arrived with dinner. As he laid out a sumptuous feast of seafood before them, he cast a disdainful glance at the napkin Grady had mauled with his pen.

"Shall I bring another napkin, sir?" he asked.

"If you would," Grady said casually, apparently thinking nothing of destroying restaurant property. He looked annoyed when the waiter went away.

"Maybe you should bring a blackboard to the restaurant next time instead of relying on the linens, Grady," a familiar deep voice said.

Jane gasped and looked up from her lobster to see Allan perched over their table, dressed in a beautiful dark gray suit, pink shirt and outlandish floral print tie that indicated he had been on another shopping spree. Sling or no sling, he was incredibly handsome.

Taking in Jane's dumbfounded expression, he grinned and widened his gray eyes as if in shock. "What a surprise to find you two here!" he exclaimed.

She glanced at him suspiciously, then looked at Grady.

He seemed to have a difficult time focusing, but when he finally did recognize Allan, he didn't appear pleased. "What are *you* doing here, Allan?"

Just then, Patricia, dressed in a slinky royal-blue number, her hair flawlessly coiffed for the evening, finally caught up with her date. She saw Allan talking to someone and put on her brightest, schmoozing grin—

which abruptly faded when she discovered Grady and
Jane were to be the undeserving recipients of her mil-
lion-kilowatt charm.

"Oh, it's you," she muttered in disappointment.

Whom had she been expecting—the Trumps?

"You don't mind if we join you, do you?" Allan
asked.

Before everyone could voice their numerous objec-
tions, Allan flagged down the maître d', who hadn't yet
noticed that he had lost his customers a few tables back
and was already hovering over a candlelit setup for two.
Patricia looked longingly at the man, and at the intimate
yet very visible table by the dance floor.

"Really, Allan," Grady protested, "this is a small
table—"

Allan waved off that concern. "Don't worry," he
said, "we won't take up much room. Patricia never orders anything more than a side salad, anyway."

The maître d', looking put out, finally backtracked to
retrieve his customers. "We'll be sitting with these people," Allan told the man. "We just need some chairs—
oh, and here are some right behind me." He turned
around two chairs from another table and scooted one
in for Patricia, whom he seated between Grady and
Jane. Then he pushed in his own on the opposite side.
"There! Isn't this cozy?"

Patricia shot everyone a long-suffering look. "Allan
just couldn't decide what he wanted to eat tonight. For
an hour and a half we've been doing nothing but going
from restaurant to restaurant, walking in several places
and then walking right out again."

Allan laughed genially. "Couldn't make up my
mind," he said innocently.

But Jane knew better. He had hunted her down—and

had done a pretty good job of it, too. She fumed silently, looking down at her uneaten lobster and feeling her hunger disappear. She glanced across the table to Grady, but her inebriated date had lapsed into a sulk.

"Well, what are we having?" Allan asked, scooting a hair closer to her.

She sent him a sideways glare.

"Mmm, everything looks just delicious," Patricia said, poring over her menu. Then she eyed Jane's lobster from across the table and wrinkled her nose a fraction—like Samantha on "Bewitched." "I always find a big plate of seafood like that so...filling, don't you?"

Jane tried to think of something to say, but Patricia laughed and waved a hand at her. "Silly of me to ask, I guess. Everyone can tell *you're* not one of those annoying calorie counters."

Jane fought the urge to bristle, knowing it was exactly what Patricia wanted.

"I *love* a woman with a healthy appetite!" Grady yelled out of the blue to no one in particular. Jane was really beginning to worry about him, especially since he had gotten hold of another of those snake drinks somewhere along the way.

Patricia sighed. "Well, I suppose an appetite is fine for women who don't have to worry about those pesky cameras. Well, take Jane for instance." Patricia sent her a saccharine smile. "Jane always looks so...healthy. Anyone can tell she doesn't deprive herself."

Allan glanced over at Jane, who was seething so furiously that she feared smoke was rising from the crown of her head. "I think she looks beautiful tonight," he said, his voice warm and husky.

Grady was practically asleep, so the table was silent for a few moments while Allan smoldered irresistibly,

Jane squirmed uncomfortably under his sexy gaze, and Patricia grew more irate.

"A camera adds ten pounds to a person's looks, you know," Patricia informed them, opening her menu again with a snap. "So I'd better not have much tonight."

"Patricia's doing the eleven o'clock newscast," Allan said.

"I really do need to get back to the station in a little bit. No time for dessert." Patricia looked up at Jane. "But you go right ahead."

Jane screwed up her lips. The only dessert she felt a need for at the moment was an old fashioned custard pie to slam right into the catty newslady's kisser.

"Would you like to dance, Patricia?" Allan asked.

Though Jane felt a jolt of envy at the idea of Patricia being in Allan's arms even for a second, she took comfort in the prospect of sitting at a Patricia-free table for at least the length of a Portuguese song. A dance would also serve the dual purpose of getting rid of Allan, which would be good. Maybe her pulse would start behaving more like a human's and less like a hamster's.

Patricia fluttered self-consciously, then admonished, "Oh, Allan, you don't like to dance!" Naturally, though, she was already rising to her feet.

"No, but I thought you might," Allan replied. "Or perhaps you'd just like a walk around the block."

Patricia's preening smile faded into faint confusion, and for the first time Jane glanced over at Allan and noted the wry grin on his lips.

"A walk?" Patricia asked. *"Now?"*

Allan smiled devilishly. "I thought it might do you some good, since you seem to be overly concerned about your weight tonight."

Her face fell. "Oh, but—"

"It would be unusual, of course, but if you would like to work off some of those calories you never take in, I'm sure everyone here would understand."

Patricia's cheeks flushed pink even beneath her healthy layer of blusher. "Well, goodness! I was *just* making conversation."

Suddenly, Grady snapped out of his Anaconda funk long enough to holler, "Dance? Did you want to dance, sweetie?"

Patricia looked from Allan to Jane to Grady in helpless confusion. "Dance?" she repeated. "Why, no, I—"

"Sure!" Grady said as the band kicked into another samba. "Thanks for asking!"

He pushed his chair back and stood, weaving precariously. Jane didn't think the man could walk, much less dance, but he surprised her by leading a perplexed Patricia out to the floor with barely a bobble.

Jane watched them, enjoying Patricia's discomfort immensely, until she felt Allan's gaze watching *her*. Slowly, she turned. "You should have been an engineer," she told him.

"Why?"

"Because you engineered this evening quite nicely."

He grinned. "I'll admit I didn't just happen to bump into you, but Grady's being soused on Pythons was your doing, not mine."

"Anacondas," she corrected. "You have the wrong snake and the wrong person to place the blame on. I don't know what's gotten into him tonight."

"Maybe he's planning to kiss you and he's trying to work up the courage."

She looked into Allan's gray eyes and felt such a

wave of desire she thought she might tip backward. *He* was the only man she wanted to kiss.

"I don't know why kissing me would take courage," she told him coolly.

"Because you seem so warm, and yet at the same time you're elusive."

She couldn't help laughing. "That's the corniest line I've ever heard!"

"But it's true," he said honestly. "You keep slipping through my fingers."

"I keep telling you *no*," she corrected, "a word you've never been happy to accept. As for elusiveness, I bet Miss 'America Alive!' out there is much more elusive than I am."

Allan sent an annoyed glance to the dance floor, where Grady was gyrating in crazy circles around Patricia, who was doing her valiant best to maintain her poise. In fact, looking at just her face no one would ever have guessed there was a man doing something resembling a whooping crane mating dance around her.

"Patricia? Elusive?" Allan asked. "On the contrary. She makes it clear to me that she's available to me every day. Practically hourly."

Jane's eyebrow shot up. She wasn't sure she wanted to hear this, yet she couldn't resist asking, "Makes it clear...how?"

"By pestering me nonstop, draping herself around me, purring suggestively at me all the time."

"Sounds like torture."

Actually, to her it did. And it seemed to be very unpleasant from Allan's point of view, too, which was all for the good. She had heard someone say once that love is sometimes the best revenge. Hopefully by throwing

Allan in Patricia's arms all the time she was proving that little chestnut to be true.

But while it was amusing to watch Allan being pestered by Patricia, and in the long run very satisfying to her sense of justice, at the moment it was a little hard to take. All right, a *lot* hard to take. She didn't want to think about how she would feel if Allan ever took Patricia up on all that availability she was offering him.

Correction. She already knew. She'd feel jealous.

Which was wrong. She knew that the first step to her recovery from Allan was to put him out of her mind. Maybe the way to do that was to have a new romance herself.

In fact, maybe she should screw up *her* courage and kiss Grady tonight.

She looked out at the dance floor, where Grady was still shaking his groove thing.

Maybe not.

"Are you really stuck on that guy?" Allan had been watching her watch Grady and must have mistaken her amused smile for fondness.

Actually, she was fond of Grady. But stuck on him? Certainly not. And she definitely wasn't in love with him. Not the way she felt about—

She stopped herself just in time. Perhaps what she really needed to do was simply recondition her mind to focus on someone else beside the dark-haired charmer at her side. And to begin, she had to convince him she was unavailable. "I know I feel something for Grady," she said evasively. "Something very special."

Allan frowned. "That's not very specific."

She laughed nervously. "Maybe it's the best I can do right now."

He looked over at the napkin Grady had been scribbling figures across. "Renting versus purchasing," he read, skimming the cloth for clues. "IRAs, housing interest deductions, Westchester... Say! This sounds serious."

"Well..." She shrugged. "You know Grady."

Allan eyed Jane suspiciously. "Has he been popping the question again?"

"Yes."

Allan crossed his good arm over his bad one and let out an exasperated sigh. "Now you see, this just isn't fair."

"Why not?"

"You keep changing the rules on me! First you say you don't want to go out with someone you work with. Then you agree to go out with Grady."

"That's different."

"I don't see why," he muttered. "Anyway, by the time I get the protocol figured out, Grady will have already whisked you away to Westchester. What does he have that I haven't?"

"It's what you *do* have that worries me more."

"What?"

She nodded to the dance floor. "Patricia." Although, at the moment, Grady had Patricia—in a precarious low-to-the-floor dip. Jane sucked in her breath and squeezed her eyes shut for a split second, fearing they were about to witness the spectacle of a local celebrity dropped to the saltillo tile.

"Oh, Allan," she said, taking pity on the very woman who five minutes ago she'd wanted to bless with a pie to the kisser. "I think a rescue is in order."

ALLAN WAS WATCHING the precarious tilt of Grady and Patricia's dip through a nervous squint just as Grady pulled his partner back up and spun her around in a wild blue twirl. The couple had drawn the attention of all the restaurant patrons now, especially the ones closest to the dance floor, who appeared poised to guard their loved ones and their dinner plates should Grady samba their way.

"Stay right here," Allan told Jane.

He got up and began picking his way through the tables toward the dance floor, where Grady and Patricia were now holding forth on their own. Grady, suddenly aware of being the floor show, began releasing exuberant Ricky Ricardo–type babaloo cries. For her part, Patricia tried several times to samba surreptitiously away, but Grady kept catching her again, spinning and dipping her in a stunning public display.

On his way to the dance floor Allan got trapped behind a waiter carrying a tray aloft, and since the tables were so tightly packed it was hard to maneuver around him. "Help is on the way!" he called out, trying to give Patricia some hope.

Several diners around him laughed, but Patricia sent him a look that was one hundred percent gratitude. Then Grady had pulled her back into his arms for the dance's grand finale. Sweat pouring off his brow, he shuffled her back and forth in a hip-grinding clinch, then, with an exuberance that could only come from a stockbroker soused enough to think he's John Travolta, he sent Patricia reeling across the floor as the little band played its last notes.

Allan hoped that he might catch his spinning date before she incurred any injuries; she was headed straight for a table of five. His left arm made it difficult to move past the waiter; instead, he ended up shoving the guy. The waiter provided a barrier between Patricia and the table, though, unfortunately, he also lost control of his tray, which held three cheesecakes and four servings of flan—all of which landed on Patricia in a direct hit.

The diners collectively gasped in surprise as the tray and glassware clattered to the floor, the waiter made his nervous apologies, and Patricia stood in shock, glazed custard dripping from her hair.

To Allan's surprise, Jane zoomed right past him, coming to Patricia's aid.

"Are you all right?" she asked, concern in her voice.

Patricia looked at her, still in a horrified daze. "I need... I need..." Just then, a dollop of cheesecake fell from her hair, and she flinched in alarm and let out a startled cry. "Oh, no! I have to get back to the station. What am I going to do?"

Bemused, Allan scratched his head. "What does Katie Couric do when she gets flan in her hair?"

The two women glared at him.

"We'll get you a cab," Jane promised, leading the stunned newswoman toward the door.

Allan went after Grady, who was still in ta-da position on the dance floor. "This way, Mr. Astaire," he said, taking his arm. Grady stumbled along beside him.

"Where's Jane?" he asked.

"Jane?" Allan repeated.

"I wanted to th-thank her for the dance," Grady slurred.

Allan rolled his eyes as they passed their abandoned table, onto which he threw enough cash to cover Grady and Jane's meals, a large tip and any damage old twinkle-toes might have caused.

Out on the street, Jane had flagged down a cab and Patricia was already darting into it. Allan went up to the driver and handed him a twenty to cover Patricia's ride. Then he looked at Grady, and a devilish idea occurred to him. He handed the man another ten and tossed Grady in the cab, too.

"You can take him home after you drop off Miss Blakemore."

"Oh, for heaven's sake!" Patricia cried in alarm, horrified to find herself in the same vehicle with the man who had already done her so much damage.

"Pat-tricia?" Grady slurred in disbelief. "You mean you're not Jane?"

"Oh!" Patricia was attempting to escape when the cab pulled into traffic at breakneck speed and whisked her and Grady off into the night.

When the cab had gone, Allan found himself facing Jane, who stood with her arms crossed and a very disapproving look on her face. God, she was beautiful. A soft breeze blew her dark, shoulder-length hair, and he found he wanted nothing more than to reach across and run his hands through it.

"It's a lovely night," he said, trying to ignore that stern glare. "Care for a stroll?"

"You shouldn't have done that."

"Done what?" he asked.

"Don't play innocent with me. You deliberately poured Grady into that cab with Patricia."

Allan shrugged guiltily. It was true. He felt a lot less kindly toward Grady since Jane had told him that she "felt something" for him. "All right, I plead guilty. And I'm also aware that I interrupted your dinner. So, to that end, I'm willing to make it up to you. Where would you like to go?"

Jane lifted her gaze toward the tops of the buildings around them as if for patience. "I can't go anywhere with you, Allan!"

"Why not?"

"I already told you—"

He lifted a finger to stop her. "No, you said you wouldn't go on a date with me," he said, correcting her. "This wouldn't be a date, because we just ran into each other."

"Just happened to, on purpose."

He smiled, and when he did, she sent him one of those strange, perplexed expressions she and so many others had worn around him so often. As if they just didn't know what to do with a smiling Allan Steele. "How about some ice cream?" he asked.

She stood rooted firmly to the pavement. "I can't. I need to get home."

"It's early yet," he told her. "And besides, I *do* owe you."

She twisted her lips into an uncertain line, hesitating. If he hadn't been sure that she would whack him upside the head with her little black purse, he would have tried to kiss the hesitation right off those beautiful lips of hers. Instead, he made do with a buddylike punch to her arm. "C'mon," he said, cajoling her. "I know a place that makes ice cream almost as good as your father and I do." He waggled his eyebrows. "And I promise not to tell Grady that you did anything fun after you guys were separated."

Finally, she laughed, giving in. "All right, just this once. But after the ice cream, I've got to hop in a cab and go straight home."

He raised his right hand. "I give you my solemn word that I'll have you home by midnight."

"Eleven," she countered.

"Oh, all right, eleven," he agreed. "At least that way

we can see if Patricia got all the flan out of her hair in time to do the newscast.''

HE WAS AS GOOD as his word, he thought proudly nearly two hours later as a cab carrying him and Jane careered across the Brooklyn Bridge. Of course, Jane hadn't wanted him to escort her home, but he had worn her down, promising to do nothing more than drop her off at her door.

He couldn't say why, but ever since he had returned from New York, Jane and ice cream had become his passions. There was no fighting it, even if he had wanted to. He even felt the same way about her after she had insisted on ordering sorbet instead of ice cream.

He shook his head. "Well, I guess I'll just have to get used to it.''

Jane, who had been gazing at the Statue of Liberty standing proudly in the harbor in the distance, snapped her head around, puzzled. "Used to what?"

"Sorbet.''

Her brow wrinkled. "What?"

He shrugged. "I suppose it's here to stay. Something that has to be dealt with.''

She laughed, making him wonder for a moment if he leaned over and kissed her whether he would be able to taste the strawberry-banana flavor lingering on her lips. "Allan, are you still thinking of starting an ice cream factory?"

"Absolutely," he said. "Your father and I—"

"Oh, no," she moaned. "You're not *really* trying to involve my father in this crazy scheme!"

"Why not?"

"Because it took me years to convince him to retire. Did you know he's almost seventy?"

"A perfect age to begin a new career."

She shook her head. "I mean it. I want him to be able to relax."

Allan chuckled. "I think what you mean is that *you* would like to relax vicariously, through your father."

"That's ridiculous."

"Oh? Somehow, I can't see you idling away on a farm when you're seventy."

She arched a brow and regarded him through green eyes that almost sparkled in the night. "How do you see me?"

"Well, for one thing, I'm sure you'll still be trying to whip everyone around you into shape. But instead of clients and co-workers, I see you surrounded by grandchildren, who probably take twice as much energy anyway." He laughed. "You might wind up on your father's farm, all right, but knowing you, it won't be relaxing."

To his delight, she was smiling. "Actually, that's not a half-bad vision. I could live with it."

"How many grandchildren do you see yourself having?"

"Oh, a bunch. What does it matter, since someone else is actually in charge of taking care of them?" She chuckled.

The cab swung onto a side street of row houses, which meant that this must be Jane's neighborhood. Allan felt his heartbeat speeding up. He couldn't let Jane get away from him. "But you know, to have all those grandkids, you've got to have your own kids first."

Her smile faded, and she looked away. He could see her hand clutching at the door handle already. "That *would* make sense," she agreed.

"Have you ever given the idea of having children any thought?"

She swung her head around, and in the streetlights as the cab came to a stop, he could see two blotches of color in her cheeks.

"This is it," the cabbie mumbled.

Jane fumbled for her purse, but Allan stopped her. "I've got it," he said, throwing a wad of bills into the plastic slot. "Keep the change," he told the cabbie as he slid across the seat and out the door after Jane.

She turned to him on the street, a look of panic on her face when she saw the cab pulling down the street. "Allan, the taxi—"

"I sent it away," he said.

"But how are you going to get home?"

"I'll take the subway."

She sent him a round-eyed, horrified stare. "The subway!"

"Why, isn't it safe?" he joked.

"Of course not," she answered matter-of-factly, walking on ahead. "And you would *never* take the subway."

He shook his head as he fell into step beside her. "Do you realize that you're still telling me what I would and wouldn't do, as if I don't exist anymore?"

"You don't," she said. "Not in the way you used to."

"Have you ever considered that this is just me now? From what I've heard about the old me, that's not such a bad thing."

"But, Allan—" She stopped at her doorstep and reached in her purse for her keys. "You must want to be yourself again. You can't just *change* all of a sudden."

He shrugged. "Why not?"

"Well, because…"

"Obviously, I was in a rut," he said. "Maybe my accident was a way of telling me to really appreciate things I hadn't stopped to think about before."

"Like what?" she asked.

"Like nighttime cab rides to Brooklyn," he said, leaning closer. "What makes you live over here?"

"It's pretty, and cheaper, and I have a view of the Manhattan skyline."

Allan looked around, puzzled. "But this block is surrounded by buildings."

"I'm on the top floor. Believe me, if you stand on tiptoe on a chair in my kitchen, the view's a real knockout."

Jane smiled whimsically, and Allan felt he might lose his mind. There was no fighting it. This woman made him light-headed, impulsive. "There's something else I appreciate now."

"What?"

"You," he said, taking her hand and pulling her to him.

He kissed her deeply, exploring her mouth at the same time his hands cupped her face, then finally got their long-desired wish to sift through her silky brown hair. He couldn't imagine anything being so soft, unless it was Jane's skin.

She made a soft whimpering sound and relaxed against him, actually moving her hands across the breadth of his chest and then upward, finally lacing them around the nape of his neck. Allan's heart slammed against his ribs as their tongues began an age-old playful dance. Jane felt so soft, smelled so good…and he *could* taste the sweet flavor of strawberries on her lips.

She felt so right in his arms, and with the sounds of the night and the traffic a few blocks distant, the city seemed to float away. There was just the two of them, in the darkness and relative quiet, together…the way he'd dreamed of but had feared would never happen. He moved his hands down her slightly arched back to her waist and pulled her closer to him, aching with desire for her.

Jane let out another low moan but pressed against his chest, lingering a moment to taste his lips once more. "Oh, no," she muttered, finally pushing away.

It made him smile to think she was as reluctant to end the kiss as he was. "Oh, yes."

"Allan, please," she said. "We can't do this."

"But we just did," he murmured in her ear.

She looked him squarely in the eye, with a determined glint that he was tempted to try to kiss away again. "You can't come up to my apartment," she told him.

He stepped back slightly. The vehemence in her words surprised him. "I wasn't going to."

"Because you—" She stopped in midprotest. "What?"

"I just wanted to kiss you," he explained, "and now I'm going to take the subway home. Like I said."

Her mouth formed a perfectly round O of surprise, and Allan shook his head. Jane must be used to some pretty wolfish behavior from men to assume that he would want to crawl into her bed after a few innocent kisses.

Well…maybe not so innocent.

"Unless you *want* me to come upstairs," he said jokingly, wriggling his eyebrows at her in his best cocktail lounge lizard impression.

"No!" she cried. "Allan, please. We should forget that kiss ever happened."

"What do you mean?"

"I mean, I'm very tired." She turned and thrust the wrong key into her door, then tried another. "I'm just going upstairs now to—"

He took her keys from her nervous, fumbling fingers, and turned the lock. When she looked at him anxiously, he pushed the door open and handed the keys back to her. "Despite my faulty memory, I just can't forget at will. And that kiss was unforgettable."

She rolled her eyes in frustration. "But don't you see? I *can't* get involved with you. You've got to accept that. Kissing is one thing, but I've got a lot more to think about than that. So good night."

Before he could say one thing to counter her words, she shut the door firmly in his face.

What on earth had gotten into the woman? he wondered, standing perplexed on her doorstep before slowly heading back down the dark street lit by periodic puddles of light from the street lamps. One minute Jane had been soft and yielding in his arms, and the next, she was back to her old prickly self, insisting they could have no relationship.

But why? Why did she seem so reluctant to give in to her attraction to him?

Was it Grady?

She had said something about having a lot going on, as if she were worried about something. Something specific. Something that would preclude a relationship with him.

He frowned, thinking. He needed to find out what

that something was. Otherwise he might actually lose Jane before he'd even reached square one with her.

But how could he find out? Jane wouldn't tell him anything. He considered hiring a private detective. But that seemed too sneaky. Too sleazy.

No. He'd tail her himself. In fact, he would start sleuthing tomorrow. Following her still didn't seem right—but then again, how else was he going to search for clues for why she thought anything more than a kiss between them was impossible?

That decided, he felt much better...until he stopped, frowning again, and looked up. He did have another problem. A very big one.

Where the heck was the subway?

Chapter Eight

She paused outside an ice cream parlor. Very interesting.

Allan hovered across the street in his brown London Fog coat, wondering if Jane would actually go inside. For his first time out sleuthing, he was doing pretty well. This morning he'd tailed her all the way from the office to that temple of the roaring twenties, the Woolworth Building, without a hitch. And now he had discovered, to his utter delight, that his Jane was apparently developing a sweet tooth for the cold creamy stuff.

He smiled, then caught her turning to look behind her, and ducked deeper into a doorway. He doubted she could see him. In true Bogart-movie fashion, the sky was sending down a steady drizzle, and people on the streets were bulked up with coats, umbrellas and hats.

Still, Jane loitered for a while in front of the shop, then walked to the doors of the Woolworth Building itself. Did she have an appointment there?

A young guy was hawking collapsible umbrellas in the overhang in front of the door, and Jane stopped to look over his wares.

"C'mon," Allan muttered to himself, "you didn't come all this way for an umbrella."

But no one would have known it from looking at her. One by one, she picked up almost every specimen the young man had on his table and examined it—almost as if she were checking for explosives. In the end, she looked at the young man, shook her head, turned on her heel and went inside the building.

Allan raced across the street, glanced into the lobby and saw her waiting for the elevator. With about five other people. Damn. How would he ever find out where she was going?

He turned to the umbrella salesman. "You see that woman in the blue trench coat?"

The kid raised an eyebrow, annoyed. "Ms. Cautious Consumer, you mean?"

"That's the one." Allan whipped out a twenty from his wallet. "She's about to get on the elevator. I'll pay you to find out where she's going."

The kid looked at him warily. "I gotta watch my stuff."

"I'll watch it, and give you another five when you come back."

The kid didn't have to be a rocket scientist to know that he was about to make more money from five minutes' work than he would in a morning of selling umbrellas. He snatched the twenty and did a hundred-yard dash to make it to Jane's elevator just as the doors were sliding closed.

Allan sighed with relief when he saw the kid slip through, then settled down in the umbrella salesman's chair. Say, this detective work wasn't so hard. If he went bust on Wall Street—which, given his lack of interest was looking increasingly likely—then couldn't get his ice-cream business off the ground, he could probably make quite a career out of sleuthing.

"How much for the green umbrella?" an old gentle-man asked Allan. It had started to rain harder, and with only a short jacket on, the man desperately needed something.

"Ten dollars?" he said, not having the faintest idea what the kid's precious stock was worth.

The man's face filled with outrage. "That's highway robbery! I'll give you five."

Some unfamiliar feeling—that financial greed that had been lying dormant back at the office—kicked in. The thrill of the bargain, of making a buck, finally over-came him. Like a fever. He wasn't about to budge. "Ten."

"Seven."

Allan clenched his jaw, then saw the man begin to close his wallet. He didn't want to lose a sale, either. "Eight," he said, compromising.

The man handed him eight bucks, scowling. "It's robbery, I tell you," he said, walking away with his purchase.

Allan was happily counting his money when the kid returned.

"Dr. Gary," he informed Allan, breathless from run-ning. "Barbara Gary."

"Great," Allan said, switching gears again, back to detective. "Here's your five bucks—and here's another eight. I sold an umbrella."

The kid shook his head. "They're only worth five, man."

Allan felt stricken. "Really?" He looked off into the distance, trying to see if he could spot the old guy in the jacket, but he was gone.

He couldn't believe he'd squeezed the old fellow for

an extra three bucks unnecessarily. And felt so gleeful doing it, too. He'd have to watch that.

"That doctor?" the kid said, trying to bring him back to his most immediate problem. "Her office is on the eleventh floor."

Allan nodded. "Thanks," he said, turning to go inside. Then he asked, "What kind of doctor is she?"

The kid shrugged. "Didn't look."

That was easily solved, Allan thought. He checked the directory in the lobby of the Woolworth Building and sure enough, under G was Barbara Gary, M.D. Then next to her name was written, Obstetrics.

Allan turned toward the elevator, then froze. Confused, he stared at the board again, certain he had been mistaken. But no, there was that word again. Obstetrics. But why would Jane be going to see an obstetrician?

Then again, why else?

"ANY CRAVINGS?" Dr. Gary asked Jane.

"Ice cream."

And Allan.

Both were his fault. He had whetted her appetite—for ice cream and for him. And no matter how much she wanted frozen sweets, it probably wouldn't match how much she craved kissing him again.

She had been so ready to forget him—had thought that by going out with Grady she had been taking a serious step in that direction. But Allan's showing up for her date had dashed that idea. Before she had known what was what, he had whisked her away, walked her to her doorstep and given her a kiss that she would never forget.

How was she supposed to ignore Allan and get on with her life when he kept popping up in it?

"Did your husband come with you today?" Dr. Gary asked.

Jane froze. "I'm not married."

Dr. Gary looked up and smiled. "That's right. Your fiancé then. You should bring him by sometime."

Jane squirmed in discomfort. "Sure."

This was only her second visit to Dr. Gary, but Jane liked the woman immensely and felt at ease—or as much at ease as possible talking to a woman who grilled her on the subject of varicose veins and hemorrhoids. Unfortunately, during the first visit, Jane had said she had a fiancé, which of course she did have at the time. But now Jane was too embarrassed to admit that no such person existed.

Maybe she just didn't want to face up to the prospect of being all alone in that delivery room quite yet. Usually she tried not to think about that day, but here in a clinical setting, surrounded by medical posters illustrating birth canals and fetal growth, it was hard to avoid the physical reality of childbirth. No one would be there to tell her to breathe, or push, or do any of the things she had seen on television or in the movies. She would have to do her breathing and pushing all by herself.

Despite these worries, however, everything was going swimmingly according to Dr. Gary, so she left the exam room slightly more upbeat. She even decided to give in to her cravings and go next door for one of those sinfully sweet ice cream cones she'd seen on the way in.

She was halfway across the doctor's waiting room when she noticed a man sitting in the corner reading a parenting magazine who looked suspiciously like Allan.

In fact, who *was* Allan! There was no mistaking his

good looks—or that sling, which was sticking out awk-wardly beneath a trench coat worn over only one arm.

Jane froze in shock, wishing she could disappear, or blend in with the baby-blue wallpaper that festooned the waiting room. How had he found out she would be here?

As if in answer to her question, Allan rose, smiling up at her as casually as if he had agreed beforehand to meet her there.

"How did it go?" he asked, as any father-to-be might have.

Cold, clammy panic set in, leaving her speechless.

Allan had no way of knowing he was an expectant father. Had their kiss jarred something in his memory? Or had he somehow guessed her condition from her behavior? Was she walking around unknowingly with the words "pregnant person" written all over her?

What the heck was going on?

"What are you doing here?" she finally asked him.

He glanced around the crowded waiting room, which Jane suddenly noticed was incredibly silent, except for the constant whistling whir of the air-conditioning. Some of the other patients peeked curiously up at them over their magazines and books. "Waiting for you, nat-urally," Allan said, attempting to take her arm and head for the door.

She dug in her heels, too spooked by his appearance to let him drag her out of the safety of the office just yet. "How did you know I would be here?"

"I followed you."

Somehow, that idea hadn't occurred to her. She had been thinking in terms of psychic connections between dads-to-be and moms-to-be. "You mean you've been *spying* on me?"

"Yes." And he seemed completely unrepentant about it.

She put her hands on her hips, her anger rising. "May I ask why?"

He looked askance at one of the peekers, and the woman immediately thrust her head back into her well-thumbed copy of *What to Expect When You're Expecting.* "I wanted to know where you were going, naturally."

"Naturally?" she asked heatedly. "Why didn't you just ask?"

"Would you have told me?"

"Probably not."

"I rest my case."

She rolled her eyes. "Who do you think you are, Perry Mason?"

"No, just someone who cares about you."

Oh God, how she wished that were true. She looked up into his eyes and remembered how hopeful she had felt once, back when they were still about to be married. She should have told him then that they were going to have a baby. She'd thought his not knowing for a while wouldn't hurt him. The irony was that she never would have guessed that by the time the sun set on her wedding day, he not only wouldn't know about her baby, but even about her, or the wedding that was to take place.

Maybe she had brought all of this upon herself by not being up-front with him to begin with. But that didn't justify his spying on her!

"Why didn't you tell me?" he asked.

What could she say now? She certainly couldn't blurt out the truth about whose baby she was having without giving the matter some thought. This new Allan might be better at emoting than the old one, but did he really care for her as anything more than a mere flirtation?

She shrugged. "I didn't want to bother you with it."

Behind her, she thought she heard a low tsking sound, but when she turned, one woman had her nose in *People* magazine and another, a woman large enough to be a ninth-monther, was studiously doing needlework.

"Don't you think it's my business?" he asked.

She fought a blush. Of course it *was* his business, but she couldn't just blurt that out now. "No," she lied. "I don't want you to concern yourself with me."

Unable to stand looking into those sincere eyes a moment longer, she ducked past him and headed straight for the door. On the way, she was snagged by a woman who looked as if she might deliver at any moment. "Swallow your pride, honey," the stranger urged her, "you'll be thankful when you get as far along as I am." Then she jabbed a thumb toward Allan and smiled. "'Sides, he's not half bad-looking."

In thanks, Allan sent the woman his broadest, sexiest grin.

Jane let out a ragged sigh that was almost a cry for help, then pushed through the door. She had to get out of there—and away from Allan so she could think!

But naturally he was right on her heels. "Jane, wait up. Will you listen to me?" When she didn't stop, he called after her, "All right, I'll see it your way!"

His words echoed in the marble hallway as she sped to the elevator and jabbed the down button. Luckily, the doors opened almost immediately on a group of businessmen and an older, craggy man wearing a tool belt, jeans and heavy work boots. The men's smiles disappeared when they saw her anxious face. She dashed into the car, hoping to evade Allan, but he was right at her elbow, and still talking.

"Didn't you hear me? If you're pregnant, it's your business," he said, ignoring the wide stares from the other men as he sidled through the cramped space to reach her.

"Stop following me," she said.

"I can't help it. I *do* feel some responsibility toward you," he said.

His speaking in such general terms was hardly comforting. Pride stinging as freshly as it had on their so-called wedding day, she lifted her chin and reminded him, "You've got Patricia."

"Oh, hang Patricia. I don't love her." He thought the matter over for a brief second and clarified, "Or at least, I don't think I do."

As the elevator doors opened to squeeze another person in, Jane noticed that the stares from the original men had become a shade more hostile. One of them even let out an animalistic grunt.

"Have you told your father?" Allan asked when the doors were closed again.

"I couldn't! He's sweet but he'd never understand."

The bell inside the car rang, signaling that they had reached the lobby. "Yeah," Allan agreed, shaking his head. "Poor old guy would probably want you to be married."

The other passengers anxiously filed out when the doors opened, all except the craggy fellow with the tool belt, who stepped over to Allan, grabbed his collar and shoved him up against the wall. Jane had barely noticed the man on her way in, but now she saw that he was a hulk, a good three inches taller than Allan—and looked as if he ate hardware for breakfast. Jane gasped and tried to tug him off Allan.

"Listen, Mr. Fancy Suit," the man growled, "*I'm* one of those old-fashioned dads, too—and if this were my daughter, I'd break your other arm!" And with that, he placed the thick lug sole of his boot right onto the top of Allan's Italian loafer and pressed down. Hard.

"Stop!" Jane cried, whacking at the man's back. She felt like a gnat doing battle with a grizzly bear. Allan's face turned white with pain.

The man let go abruptly and disappeared into the lobby and out on the street, leaving Allan to hobble off the elevator. "I don't get it," he muttered. "I was a hero back in your doctor's office."

"He must have misunderstood," Jane said, feeling terrible. "Are you all right?"

Allan leaned back against the wall and smiled ruefully. "I might be walking like Quasimodo for the next few decades, but I suppose things could be worse. *You're* the one I'm worried about."

She shook her head. It was all so confusing, she felt she needed time just to clear her head. Alone. But Allan wasn't going to leave her alone now.

"We'd better be getting back," she said.

He looked at her, a little dazed still. "Back to where?"

"The office," she said. "Remember, that place where you go from nine to five so you can afford to put caviar on the table?"

He released a tired breath. "Why do you insist on changing the subject?"

"Because you have an important meeting with Clyde Simington this afternoon."

His mouth curled in a way that let her know that he

couldn't have cared less about Simington. "Forget Clyde. I want to know who the father of your baby is."

Jane lifted her chin stubbornly. "You just said that was my business."

"No, I said the *baby* was your business. I personally would like to get my hands on the father and shake some sense into him."

"Me, too," Jane said, withholding a bitter smile.

"Then who is it?"

"No one."

His eyes widened. "That's impossible."

"No, it's not," she answered heatedly. "Plenty of women have babies by themselves, and I'm going to be one of them."

Allan's face reddened and for a moment she thought he was going to step out and squish *her* foot. "A kid needs a stable home."

"I can give him that."

"Wouldn't a father be a nice addition to this scenario?"

"Better to have no father than a father who's a heel," she argued. She didn't want to be having this discussion, period. "Now about your meeting with Clyde..."

"Him again."

"Yes, him. You've been trying to get your hands on his portfolio for months, Allan. Even I've had dinner with the man, who by the way is quite charming. And I've worked everything up so you don't even need to—"

"Okay, okay," Allan said, giving up. "I get the picture. You're not going to tell me any more about the father of your baby, and it's time to go kowtow to the rich and famous." He took her by the elbow and led her to the door.

It was still so unbelievable to hear Allan saying things like that—Allan, who just weeks ago had practically lived, eaten and breathed Clyde Simington. And as for the father of her baby...

She steadfastly refused to look at Allan during the cab ride back to the office. It wasn't far, but she could feel tension inside that car thick enough to cut with a knife. Even so, she was preoccupied. Allan's sudden appearance at the doctor's office made her think. Though she didn't trust him enough to get involved personally with him again, *should* she tell him about the baby? It *was* his, after all. And a person deserved to know when he was going to be a father...

The old Allan she had feared telling because she had thought he wouldn't care—in fact, she'd worried that he would call off the wedding. But the new Allan was so much the opposite. There was no guessing what he would do. Or whether he might not return to his senses and react like the old Allan after all.

But if a kiss didn't jar his memory, she thought a little peevishly, and neither did learning she was having a baby, what would?

One thing was certain. *She* was going to have to raise a child, Allan or no Allan, and to do so effectively she needed to rely on herself and maybe Dr. Spock, not a devilish charmer with a big ego and a faulty memory. She needed to stay not only physically healthy, including cutting down on her worry by trying to forget Allan, she needed to be financially sound so that she could be a good provider. And since it was increasingly clear that she was not getting anywhere in her job search, that meant becoming more secure in the job she did have.

And telling the boss you were having his baby didn't seem a smart thing to do, job security-wise.

The cab dropped them off outside their building, but when they got out, Allan stopped at the revolving glass door of the building. "You go on ahead," he said.

Jane regarded him nervously. He'd been quiet on the way back from her doctor's, which was uncharacteristic of Allan. Of the new Allan. "Are you going out to lunch?"

"No," he said, "I'm going out to think."

WHO? WHO WAS THE FATHER of Jane's baby?

The more Allan mulled over the question, the more perplexed he became, although some things at least became clear in his head. Like why Jane wasn't interested in having a relationship with him. Poor thing had probably just been ill-used by some other man—a man who was either so uncaring that he didn't want to face up to his responsibilities, or someone so detestable that Jane wouldn't tell him he was going to be a father. Also, Jane was too honorable to feel she could become involved with a man without telling him she was going to have another man's baby.

Allan went back to the counter and ordered another scoop of cherry vanilla, which was surprisingly good. He would have to take a sample for Will the next time he went to Vermont.

Will. He wondered what *he* was going to make of all this. Or whether, being the astute old bird that he was, he actually knew of Jane's condition already. Allan was tempted to run back to the office and call Vermont.

But no. This was Jane's business. Jane's...and someone else's.

Who?

He wasn't sure why the father question affected him so sharply. But when she had mentioned having the baby all on her own, something inside him had rebelled at the thought. He had gathered enough information about himself to know that he had grown up mostly in foster homes, one after another—so he couldn't have been very happy as a kid. Maybe that was why the "old" Allan Steele sounded like such a thrill to be around. Why he'd lived in an apartment with no pictures, no color, and had chased after a woman who had no heart. And maybe that explained the little pain he'd felt when Jane had mentioned her fatherless child. A kid needed all the help he could get coming into this world.

Not to mention Jane deserved a little help herself, whether or not she decided to marry the fellow.

She had only given him one clue as to the man's identity. *"Better to have no father than a father who's a heel,"* she'd said. And maybe her thinking was right.

Still, he wanted to figure out the identity of this mysterious heel.

He began systematically going through men Jane had contact with. But he knew of so few. The most obvious candidate was Grady. He knew that his partner had been pestering Jane for quite some time, and that she had ambivalent feelings about him. But was Grady the heel?

It didn't seem likely. For one thing, from what Allan had witnessed, Grady might be annoying, but he wasn't quite detestable. And besides, it was no secret that Grady *wanted* to marry Jane. Was dying to, as a matter of fact. Besides, as much as Grady pestered Jane, Allan wasn't certain the two had actually spent much time together, or had even dated before last night at Rio's. And that hadn't worked out too well.

So that would seem to take care of Grady.

There were a few other men about the office, callow

youths whom he couldn't imagine Jane giving a second glance. Obviously, he couldn't be ruling out anyone at this point, but he was fairly certain the person he was looking for had to be someone Jane admired, someone she had spoken of often....

Almost immediately, a light bulb went off in his head. Then, the more he thought about it, bells and whistles sounded. And wailing alarms. It was so obvious—why hadn't he thought of it before?

Clyde Simington!

Allan shot out of his chair and looked at his watch. Ten till twelve—the hour when he was supposed to have his meeting with Simington. He had become so obsessed with his Jane problem that he'd almost forgotten.

Simington was the Connecticut granite king Jane hadn't stopped talking about since the moment Allan had been roused back to consciousness in the hospital. Allan had read a little of the file on the multimillionaire and discovered that he was nearly fifty—old for Jane but not unheard of. Especially since the man had married and divorced three times, his most recent wife being a college student who had been working as a barmaid when he met her. Which proved that Simington was not above preying on younger women.

And then, Jane had an obvious fondness for the man. She often talked reverently about his portfolio; now Allan wondered whether that reverence wasn't hiding something else. Like love.

Charming, she'd called him.

She had mentioned going out to dinner with the man, too. Had a business dinner turned amorous...or into a wrestling match at a fancy suite at the Plaza Hotel?

Allan's blood began to boil just thinking of Jane being ill-used that way.

Suddenly he was walking—no, practically sprinting—back to the office. Trying to make it back in time for the meeting he had viewed so cavalierly before. He wanted to see Jane and Simington together. Then he would know the truth.

GRADY CLEARED his throat and glanced around his office uncomfortably. After his disastrous bender the night before and dragging in late this morning, the poor man appeared in no shape to face off with one of the richest men in Connecticut.

And there was no reason why he should, Jane thought, a little heatedly. Simington was Allan's pet client, a man whose portfolio Grady only had the most passing knowledge of. He was Allan's responsibility, not Grady's.

But since when did Allan—either of him—care about something so mundane as responsibility? The old one had left her holding the bouquet in front of a houseful of relatives, and his new incarnation cared about nothing but ice cream and spying on her.

She fumed silently, still uncomfortable from her encounter with Allan this morning at her doctor's office. What right did he have to come barging into her life anyway? Of course, he actually had a very important right, but what right did he *think* he had?

"To tell you the truth," Simington was saying, "I'm rather glad Mr. Steele isn't here right now."

"Glad?" Jane asked. She'd always liked the man, though he was the overly cautious type and a bit on the nervous side. Of course, he had been taken for a ride by more than one fortune hunter, so perhaps he had good reason to be cautious. On a professional basis, he had always treated her with strictest courtesy, even though he knew that she was technically just Allan's right-hand man and had no important clients of her own.

He cleared his throat. "Meaning no disrespect," he said anxiously, "the man always seemed a little sour to me, the few times I met with him. Know what I mean?"

He looked from Jane to Grady with something akin to fear in his eyes, as if he'd just been too bold. He was holding a mug of coffee, and his hand shook, making the hot liquid slop dangerously close to the brim.

"I know he worked hard trying to work up a dynamic plan for your assets," Jane assured the man.

"Well…"

Really, it was hard to be completely patient with a man who was taking more than two months just to decide whether he wanted to change brokers or not.

"Some of the investments Mr. Steele's recommended just don't seem quite square to me," Clyde hazarded to say.

"Square?" Grady asked, wincing as he took a gulp of V8. He didn't like it when people used nonprofessional lingo.

"I think Mr. Simington means they sound high-risk." Jane smiled at the man.

To her surprise, he positively beamed back. "Sure, that's what I mean. That's just what I mean! Thank you."

"What investments have you worried, Mr. Simington?" she asked.

"All that South American stuff." He frowned. "How am I supposed to know what's going on down there?"

Jane and Grady exchanged glances. "I'm sure Allan

only wanted to give your portfolio some balance. Right, Grady?''

Grady grimaced. He was in bad humor today...and after the fiasco at the Brazilian restaurant, he had little patience with Allan—or South America. "I've always told Allan that he overemphasizes Third World investments."

"But that doesn't mean we have to," Jane told Simington. "Now if you'll just look at some adjustments I've made, I think you'll see we can increase your yield significantly without incurring more risk than you're comfortable with."

She got up to show the man what she meant, but her sudden movement caught him off guard, and he jumped about two feet in the air. When his backside again made contact with chair, his lap was covered in coffee.

"Oh, I'm sorry!" Jane said, reaching for a napkin to wipe him off.

The poor man appeared as flustered as if he'd spilled coffee on her. "No, *I'm* sorry," he said, trying to take the napkins from her. The two engaged in a tug-of-war until Simington, gathering strength from his embarrassment, pulled so hard that she fell into his lap.

"Oh my goodness!" Simington cried. "Watch out!"

In a moment, Jane understood that he meant that she should watch out for her backside making contact with the coffee on his lap. Unfortunately, she didn't quite put it all together until Clyde indelicately slapped a napkin on her rear end.

Allan *would* choose that precise moment to show up for the meeting. She saw him when he appeared at the door, practically panting, his face as foreboding as a thundercloud.

"Allan," she said, hopping out of their client's lap.

Simington's head snapped around, his slightly buggy eyes practically popping out of their sockets when they saw Allan's disapproving scowl.

"I see you started without me."

Simington cleared his throat uncomfortably and crumpled the napkin in his hand self-consciously. "We were, uh...well, were..."

Grady took a deep breath, and downed another slug of V8. "We were just talking about your penchant for high-risk, high-yield investment," he informed Allan stiffly.

"Clyde wants to nix the South Americans," Jane put in. She didn't sit down, but stood to the side of Mr. Simington.

Allan plopped down into the chair next to their potential client and gave him a brief head-to-toe evaluation—a study that made poor Clyde practically writhe in discomfort. Allan apparently didn't like what he saw. "Really? I would have thought a man like you would appreciate South America. The culture of machismo, and all that."

"Machismo?" Clyde asked, his voice barely a squeak.

Jane felt a prickly dread at the edge in Allan's tone. Why was he talking about machismo in reference to Clyde? The man had more Don Knotts in him than Don Juan.

Clyde shifted uncomfortably. "Well, naturally, I have nothing against Latin America," he said. "I—I suppose I could go either way."

"I see you're a man of firm convictions," Allan said, a tad too snidely.

"Well, now, see here—"

"Allan, I was just telling Mr. Simington about the

Brazilian restaurant we visited last night," she said, trying to change the subject.

"Sounded like quite a place," Simington said, glad to be on a more even conversational plane. "I'll have to remember it the next time I'm in town."

"I bet you come to town often," Allan said. "And probably alone?"

Simington laughed anxiously under Allan's vaguely hostile stare. "Well, if I don't have a friend along."

Allan's eyebrows shot up, and he aimed his gaze at Jane. "A lady friend?"

"Well, naturally, sometimes..." He blinked. "What do you mean by 'lady friend'?"

What was Allan getting at?

"I'll bet if a man like you doesn't have a female friend in the city, he can always try to round one up," Allan said, his lip practically curling. "This city is filled with innocent, unsuspecting women who could fall prey to a man with millions."

"Say, now," Clyde protested.

Allan stood, and began pacing. Grady mumbled a warning to his partner, but Allan turned to Simington and said, "Don't tell me you've never picked up a girl in town...maybe one you have a slight business acquaintance with...wined and dined her, and led her on with false promises?"

Allan shot Jane a brief, smug glance, as if to nudge her and say, "I'll take care of this."

As understanding dawned, Jane felt her cheeks flood with heat. Allan was grilling Simington because he thought that *he* was the father of her baby! She looked over at confused, befuddled Clyde and wasn't sure whether she should laugh or give Allan a thump on the head.

"I'm not sure I get your drift, son," Simington said.

Allan rocked on his heels. "Son?" he asked mockingly. "You throw that word around awfully casually, but I wasn't aware that you had any children."

Jane shot out of her chair. "Allan, you're looking feverish. Why don't you come with me and I'll scrounge up an aspirin for you." She tugged on his arm to no avail.

Simington stood. "I don't have children, but I don't understand what any of this has to do with South American investment."

One of Allan's eyebrows arched up. "Maybe there just aren't any children you know of. Or care to know of."

Jane thought she might keel over on the spot. "Did I say aspirin? I think we might be able to round up something stronger for you."

"Like a straitjacket, maybe!" Grady agreed.

Simington, red-faced, was mere inches away from Allan, finally sputtering with rage. "I don't know what you're insinuating, Mr. Steele—"

Allan snorted. "I think you do."

The granite magnate practically raised himself on tiptoe in outrage. "But if you want to know my decision on this matter, there is no way I would let a man of your...your ilk have a hand in my money."

"You're a fine one to talk about ilk!" Allan raved self-righteously, digging his grave a little deeper.

"Allan..." Jane warned.

"Don't defend him," Allan told her.

Simington tossed up his hands, and no wonder. "The man's mad!" he said to Grady. He turned to leave.

Grady, seeing dollar signs about to walk out the door,

ran after him. "Please, Mr. Simington—Clyde—I'm sure we can work something else out."

Simington turned. "Oh, I've got it worked out, all right. No one here has a lick of sense—"

Grady was practically groveling. "Please, if you'll just—"

"—except Miss Fielding," Simington said. "Now if you'll put her in charge of my assets, then we'll have something to talk about."

Grady turned and stared at Jane with wonder. *"Jane?"*

"Of course!" Simington said. "She's got more savvy and good sense than the rest of you put together. And she's not crazy!"

Grady hesitated only momentarily, then agreed, "Of course, if that's what you want, we'll put Jane on your account. No reason why we shouldn't," he said, clapping the older gentleman on the back. "Here, I'll walk you to the elevator. Jane's always been one of our most promising up-and-comers...."

As Grady followed Simington out the door, he turned to give Jane the thumbs-up sign, and then glared once more at Allan before turning away.

After they had gone, Jane felt almost light-headed. After all that tension, her anger at Allan suddenly seeped away. Had what she thought just happened really taken place? Had the most prized client—the one Steele and Grimly had been chasing for months—just been dropped in her lap? Suddenly, she felt like jumping for joy.

"I can't believe it," she said a little breathlessly.

She turned and saw the reason why she didn't actually do a happy little jig. Allan. He was staring at her so inscrutably, almost accusingly.

"I suppose it's the least the man could do."

If Allan had slapped her, she couldn't have been more shocked. "What?"

He shrugged. "I suppose since Simington won't take direct responsibility for his actions, the least he could do was ensure you a secure income."

Jane put her hands on her hips—mostly to keep from landing a disfiguring blow to Allan's classically chiseled nose. "For your information, Allan, you're wrong if you think Simington is the father of my child. In fact, you're so wrong it would be funny if you hadn't just made such a confounded fool of yourself!"

His eyes registered surprise. "You mean you and he never…"

"Of course not!" She shook with indignation. "Where would you get such a crazy idea?"

"You've talked about him so much, and I couldn't think of anyone else."

"And so you jumped to the conclusion that I had let myself be seduced by Mr. Simington?"

"You called him Clyde before," Allan reminded her.

"I don't care if I called him cupcake! Not that it's any of your business, but you might have asked me first before you made such a scene. And as for my not deserving his account…"

He held up his hand. "I never said—"

"You said the only reason he had given it to me was because he wanted to provide for me." Her pride was still stinging over that. Maybe because hearing someone speak of her in glowing terms of savvy and good sense was so refreshing—and so far from how she had behaved with Allan. And maybe because she wanted Allan, who had been her mentor all these years, to assume that when she was awarded something like this, it was for a job well done.

"Well for your information, Mr. Simington values me because while you were pining after Patricia, I was keeping in contact with him for you. And these past few days, while you've been whipping up ice cream in the company kitchen—along with wild theories about who I might have slept with—I've been doing some work!"

Allan's expression was contrite. "Jane, you must know that I never—"

She held up her hand to cut him off, a gesture she had learned from him so well. "Never mind, Allan," she said. "No matter what your opinion is, I'm happy about the Simington account. I'm only sorry it's taken me five years of working with you to see what your real opinion of me and my abilities is."

With that, she turned on her heel and left him standing, alone and dumbfounded, in Grady's office. And despite the fact that she had landed her first big account at Allan's expense, she couldn't help but feel a little glee. Just a little.

Really, it seemed only fitting. After all, she was working her way up the corporate ladder now to support her—and his—child.

Chapter Nine

Okay, so he'd made a slight blunder.

It had been an honest mistake. He couldn't help it if he had been suspicious of Simington. After his morning at the doctor's office with Jane, what else was he to think? Especially when he walked into the office to find them in such a strangely compromising position.

After a day's reflection, Allan was willing to admit that just the idea of Jane sleeping with another man was enough to make him wild with jealousy; wild enough to jeopardize his own career and, as Jane so rightly put it, make a confounded fool of himself. He feared the scene—and Jane's wrong assumption that he thought she didn't deserve success—were going to end his tenuous hold on a relationship with her as well.

This morning when he had come into work, her old cubicle had already been emptied out. After talking to Simington, Grady had decided that he was going to give Jane a long overdue promotion. As promised, he had finally wooed Jane to his side of the office—down the long, jagged hallway that separated Steele from Grimly. Allan was happy for her, but glum that he would have fewer excuses now to see her during the day.

He sighed, tapping his pencil against his desk. Without Jane there, he felt completely rudderless. And he was still distracted by the mysterious identity of her baby's father.

A knock sounded at his door, and he looked up, hoping that Jane would be there. But it was Grady.

Looking impossibly smug as he sank down in a leather chair across the huge mahogany desk, Grady smiled. "Well, I suppose you'd better start searching for another right-hand man."

"I should have years ago, I suppose." Which was true. What had he been thinking, letting Jane languish in a junior position for so long?

Grady drummed his fingers against the arms of the chair. "Are you certain you're feeling all right? I mean...after yesterday, you might consider taking a few days off. Relax. I don't know if you realize it, but you were talking off your head, old man. Weird things about Simington's having children, things I couldn't understand."

Allan narrowed his gaze on Grady. He still hadn't cleared him completely from his list of suspects. "Haven't you ever thought about having children, Grady?"

His eyes widened in horrified response to the sudden question. "Why, not really. Such an expense!"

"All good things in life cost money," Allan told him.

Grady looked aghast. "No, no, no. 'Good things' are items like cars and Cuisinarts. *Those* cost money. Children suck you dry." When Allan laughed, Grady went on, "Just look at college. Do you know how much a Harvard education is going to cost in the year 2015?"

"How much?"

"*Modern Money* magazine estimated as much as

eighty thousand dollars a year,'' Grady said. "And that's not including books!"

"You don't say."

"Children are a bad bet, investment wise," Grady assured him. "Very bad return."

Good thing he wasn't Jane's mystery father, Allan thought. At least, he hoped he wasn't.

"Say, you haven't developed a hankering to nest, have you?" Grady asked. "I thought only women had the biological clock thing going."

"I think being around babies, or at least pregnant women, sometimes triggers an urge to nest in men, don't you?"

"No, not partic—" Grady's mouth snapped closed and he watched Allan closely for a few moments. "You've been around a woman who's pregnant?"

Allan looked at him suspiciously. He didn't know whether to take the question at face value...or whether Grady was trying to feel out how much *he* knew about Jane. Might Jane have confided in Grady? "Actually, I have," Allan said.

"Hmm." Grady studied his nervously twiddling thumbs for a moment before looking Allan in the eye again. "Are you involved with this woman?"

Allan considered for a moment. If Grady was aware of Jane's situation, it wouldn't hurt to stake his claim. Maybe that way Grady would stop pressing his suit so persistently. Then again, if Grady had no idea what he was talking about, maybe he could keep his answer oblique enough that Grady couldn't figure out the woman's identity. "You could say that."

It wasn't *entirely* a lie. He felt emotionally involved with Jane...even if she didn't want him to be.

"I see," Grady said. "I guess that explains a lot."

"A lot of what?"

He shrugged, then stood. "Your behavior lately. The distraction, the ice cream...the peculiar scenes with very wealthy clients."

Allan smiled, watching Grady back toward the door with a nervous grin on his face. The man obviously found children so distasteful he wasn't even interested in talking over the subject. He looked as if he might flee the room by breaking into a run at any moment, as though fatherhood were catching. He ran his fingers through his blond hair. "I suppose I should congratulate you."

Allan's smile disappeared. He didn't want Grady blurting this out to the entire world.

"Actually, old man," he told Grady, "we're trying to keep this under wraps. You know, she wouldn't want it to damage her career." He thought Grady would respect someone's wishes for discretion from a financial angle, at least. "So if you don't mind keeping it a secret, I'd really appreciate it."

"Don't worry about me," Grady assured him eagerly as he crept ever closer toward the door. "My lips are sealed. I'll take this to my grave."

"That probably won't be necessary," Allan told him. "Unless you plan on dying in the next nine months."

Grady laughed. "You always could think of a good zinger, Allan. Well, I'd better be going. Nose to the grindstone and all that..."

After he ducked away, Allan felt fairly upbeat. Clearly the idea of becoming a dad horrified Grady, so he doubted he and Jane would be getting married if he was the father. In fact, he doubted Grady would be going anywhere near Jane or any other woman for the next nine months.

"YOU'LL NEVER BELIEVE this," Grady said in a feverish whisper after dashing into Jane's office and shutting the door behind him.

She had been absorbed in the task of fastening her old bulletin board to the wall of her new office, but when Grady came in, her attention was fully diverted. The man was so excited, he was almost quivering. "What is it?"

"Allan and Patricia Blakemore are going to have a baby!"

For a moment, she feared the heavy bulletin board was going to slip right out of her fingers. "Did you say Allan and *Patricia?*" she asked, knowing she sounded like a nincompoop. There was no mistaking what she had heard.

"Yes!" Remembering his manners, Grady gave her a hand so that she could drive a nail into the wall.

She did, and nearly drove the hammer and her arm through the wall, too. "Are you sure he said Patricia?"

She couldn't believe it. Maybe Grady was somehow mixed up and Allan had been talking about *her.*

But Grady nodded adamantly. "Allan said that they were expecting a child, but that they had been trying to keep it a secret, because Patricia is so concerned about her career. You know yourself how obsessed that woman is with her job at the network.

"And not only that, but I think they're already planning to send it to Harvard, because Allan seemed particularly interested to know how much it would cost to go there by the time the kid was of age."

Jane felt her face flame with embarrassment. Here she had been harboring feelings for Allan, and carrying his child, and all the while he had probably been mapping out his own future with Patricia, and *their* baby. What a fool she was!

Last night she had stayed up late trying to glean some comfort from Allan's erratic behavior yesterday. She'd wondered if the scene he had caused had masked some feeling for her. Did his behavior with Simington show that he was concerned for her well-being, or just prove that all he was interested in was foisting her off on someone else? After all, he had several times referred to the "responsibility" he felt for her.

Apparently, responsibility was *all* he felt. The irony was, he should have felt twice as much responsibility as he did.

She gave herself a swift mental kick, then grew angry all over again. Last night she had considered telling Allan the whole truth, thinking she would feel guilty for having his baby right under his nose without telling him he was the father.

Ha! One thing Allan didn't lack, apparently, was paternal opportunity.

"Isn't this incredible?" Grady said. "If you had told me a month ago that Allan Steele was going to be a daddy, I would have called you crazy."

The irony was, Jane *could* have told Grady a month ago that Allan was going to be a daddy. Now she couldn't. She would never let anyone know the father's identity.

What was she going to do? She wanted to run as far away as possible, or at least to Vermont. She couldn't stick around Steele and Grimly—somebody was bound to figure out she was pregnant eventually and piece together the truth. But how could she leave now, when she was finally getting somewhere professionally?

"That's probably why Patricia came back from Paris

so soon," Grady idly mused, sinking down in her desk chair and giving it a spin. "Why she went crawling back to Allan as fast as she did."

Yes. Which meant that Patricia was probably about as far along as she herself was. Jane practically writhed with shame at the position she was in. It was like being the back-street castoff in one of those old movies she saw sometimes on television—the black and white ones that featured a rich man who has a fling with a girl from the wrong side of the tracks before being convinced by his snooty parents to give her up and settle down with a suitable girl. Those melodramas invariably ended with the poor girl winding up "in trouble," and having to do "the honorable thing." Which usually meant giving up her baby and then hurling herself off a bridge.

And now here she was. In trouble, as they used to say. And Allan was about to marry his suitable match. Only she didn't feel like flinging herself off a bridge.

She would have preferred to fling Allan.

"Well, I guess that's it for you two," Grady said.

Jane froze. "Who two?"

"You and Allan."

Jane didn't want to do anything that would indicate how upset she was. She worked hard to make her shrug seem nonchalant, though the thin foam shoulder pads in her dress felt like twenty-pound weights. "That's been over since Vermont."

He watched her closely. "I don't know...sometimes I sensed something going on between you two. I even thought maybe he had shown up at the restaurant the other night because he'd come looking for you."

Jane turned away, fiddling nervously with the little plastic box of pushpins on her desk. "Don't be silly."

"Hmm," Grady said, practically twitching with doubt.

"It was just coincidence—or maybe not. You did pick one of the hottest spots in town to take me," she said, attempting to flatter him out of his suspicions. "Maybe some of your good taste in restaurants wore off on him."

Her flattery pleased Grady. Too much.

Suddenly, he dropped to his knees. "Oh, Jane, why don't you go ahead and marry me?" he begged. Though her office was bigger than what she was used to, it was still cramped, and she felt pinned by all the furniture and boxes, not to mention Grady's firm grip on her thighs.

He looked at her pleadingly. "I was just reading a feature article in the *Journal* about Wall Street couples—they had pictures and everything. We could be one of them, Jane. Can't you see it? 'Jane and Grady Grimly—Profit and Romance in the Heart of the Metropolis.'"

Jane winced, and continued trying to pry herself away from him. "Grady, please—"

"We would be an investment dream team, the envy of everyone."

"Grady," she lectured, "there's more to marriage than joint bank accounts."

"Like what?"

She rolled her eyes. "Like love."

"I do love you!" he cried, a little too loudly. Jane glanced anxiously at the door as Grady amended, "Well, as much as I can love anyone. Dr. Winkel says I have an intimacy barrier because my parents were away so much of the time."

"I didn't know that," Jane said. "Did they travel often?"

"Yes, every evening they went to Twenty-one for cocktails."

She sighed in exasperation. "Grady, please. I can't marry you right now. My life is in flux."

"That's the perfect time to get married!" he argued. "Then when it settles down again, it will be settled for good. If you wait till things are on an even keel, then decide to marry me, you'll just be in flux again."

She had to admit, the argument had a twisted kind of logic to it. Grady was quick on his knees.

Her mind, on the other hand, was still trying to wrap itself around the idea of Allan and Patricia having a baby. Together. After Allan's little speech about babies needing stability, she had little doubt that he and Patricia would be getting married soon. Unlike herself, Patricia wouldn't be in that delivery room, breathing all alone.

"I'm sorry, Grady, I just can't make a commitment like that right now. And to be honest, I don't know if I ever will."

Looking completely dejected, Grady let go of her, restoring the circulation in her legs. Slowly, he rose to his feet. "Oh, all right," he said gloomily, dusting nonexistent lint off his expensive pants. "I guess this will give me something to talk to Dr. Winkel about this week. At least I'll get my money's worth."

"You're a good sport, Grady," Jane said, patting him reassuringly on the back as he moped toward the door, and left her alone. Finally.

Once he was gone, she almost wished him back. Without Grady there distracting her, her mind focused solely on Allan and Patricia. She went on decorating her new office, but she had little of her previous gusto for the task.

After a quarter hour of solid brooding, someone knocked, and she turned around to see a beautiful bouquet of flowers filling her door. The scent of roses wafted quickly through the little room, which was enlivened immediately by the eclectic spray of color.

Brightening, Jane dashed over to exclaim over the elaborate bouquet, when suddenly she saw Allan's face peeking over a bird of paradise. She stopped so fast her heels made sparks. She hadn't expected to see *him*. Though she didn't know why. He was still the boss.

"Congratulations!" he said.

It was on the tip of her tongue to congratulate *him* for his impending fatherhood, but then she remembered it was a secret. It was a wish she of all people should honor.

"Thank you," she said.

Allan breezed past her unbidden and placed the bouquet on her desk. "Looks nice, if I do say so myself."

That was an understatement. It looked fantastic. "A little out of place, maybe." She laughed. "But thank you. They're beautiful. They belong somewhere grand—in a Park Avenue matron's foyer."

Allan smiled. "If I were a flower, I would rather be in a workaholic's shoebox office than on Park Avenue."

"Why?"

"Because the workaholic needs me more."

"But she's going to have to shove you into a corner so she can actually sit at her desk," Jane said.

Allan looked at her in mock offense. "Do I look like I would be such an egotistical flower that I would mind being moved?"

Jane couldn't help giggling. Or help keeping her anger and resentment toward the man from slipping away. With Allan like this, it was sometimes hard to remember the way things used to be in the office, back when he was a barracuda. The terrible thing was, she had grown to care for this infuriatingly charming new incarnation almost as much as she had for the old cranky one. And now he belonged, irrevocably, to someone else.

Patricia. The woman he had always belonged to, she supposed, though she had tried for so long to deny it. She herself had just been a short interlude in his life. An emotional pit stop.

Her smile faded abruptly. "Well, thanks for bringing them by."

"You've already thanked me," Allan said. "Besides, it's I who should be thanking you for keeping me going all these years. Especially this past week."

She waved off his gratitude, wishing he, too, would go away. Wishing his voice still didn't make her insides turn to liquid. "That's what you were paying me for."

"But you've saved my hide—probably more than I can remember. I know you were trying to rescue me valiantly yesterday, only I wouldn't let you."

"Let's forget about it," she said tightly.

"Can you?" he asked, his eyes sparking seriously. "I'm amazed at the way you can behave so coolly when you have so much responsibility on your shoulders."

She fought the pang of desire she felt when she looked into his eyes. She needed to think of Allan as firmly belonging to someone else. Forbidden territory. No more late-night fancies, what-ifs, or but-maybes. He was bound to Patricia now.

"It's not so much," she said. "I'm not the first single parent this country's seen, you know."

"No, and I'm sure if anyone can make a go of it, you can."

"Thanks."

"And I want you to know, if you need time off, it won't be a problem. I can clear it with Grady, too."

The thought of the two of them discussing this panicked her. "No!" she cried. At his alarmed look, she said, "I mean, I was going to inform Grady myself. Later."

"Oh, so he isn't aware...."

"No."

He looked thoughtful for a moment, then shrugged. "I'd wondered. Well, however you want to handle it," Allan said. "I just wanted you to know that I understand the pressures on you right now."

He would. Probably Patricia had given him an earful; she wasn't one to suffer in silence.

"That's kind of you," she said, trying to hold back tears. She shouldn't cry anymore over Allan, either. Besides, she'd read all about crying in her pregnancy book. Expectant mothers felt weepy because the surge in hormones made their tear ducts seem full.

She just *felt* like crying. She didn't actually need to.

Allan stood silently watching her for a moment. For once, he looked slightly uncomfortable. But what more was there to say?

"I hope you've forgiven me for yesterday," he told her. "I behaved like a bear, and I'm very sorry."

In the wake of her promotion, and especially after the news about Patricia's pregnancy, Allan's sins of yesterday seemed very minor. "Of course," she said.

"No hard feelings?" he asked.

She smiled, trying like hell not to think about when

he'd kissed her, or worse, when they'd made love. "No hard feelings."

This would probably be the end of their relationship, she thought wistfully. No more flirtation, or midafternoon ice cream tastings, or other such silliness. Now that the news was getting out about Patricia, Allan probably wouldn't be as free and easy as he had been these past few weeks. In fact, Jane expected that being bound to Patricia for life might be just the thing that would make his sour old personality return.

"So…" Allan rocked back on his heels, looking at her face assessingly.

"So…" she repeated, feeling awkward again. Why didn't he leave?

It didn't take her long to find out.

"So…would you like to go out to dinner?"

Jane was aghast. *"Us?"* she asked, her voice rising so high it was practically a dog whistle.

He grinned. "That's usually what 'you and me' adds up to."

She stared at him long and hard. Stunned. She couldn't believe her ears!

Had Allan turned into such a skirt-chaser that he was going to keep pestering her to go out with him even after he knew Patricia was carrying his child?

"Do you mean to tell me that you're asking me out on a *date?*"

"Well, dinner," he clarified, still smiling. "But if you'd like to think of it as a date, that's certainly fine with me."

The unmitigated nerve of the man! He probably thought she didn't know about Patricia's baby yet. After all, Grady said they were attempting to keep it on the QT for now. But honestly! That didn't give him license to run around asking women out. Another pregnant woman, no less!

He looked at her, his eyes uncertain. "Have I said something wrong?"

She sputtered incoherently for a moment, just managing to bite back a remark about Patricia. Had she ever misjudged his character! The man was shameless.

"I certainly will not go out with you," she answered firmly. "Tonight or any other night."

His smile disappeared, and he looked down at her, a little perplexed. "The other night, I thought we got along pretty well."

She thought of their kiss in her doorway and felt herself go a little weak-kneed just at the memory. But she fought against that weakness. To think he had kissed her after shoving poor Patricia into a cab with drunken Grady! Was that any way to behave toward the woman who was going to bear his child?

The *other* woman who was going to bear his child, she thought, getting steamed up all over again.

"I told you that night that we couldn't go out again," she reminded him coldly.

"And it didn't make any sense to me then, either," he replied.

"Well, maybe you should go back to that penthouse of yours and give it some deep thought. The reason might come to you, sooner or later." *Or in about seven months.*

He held out his arms in supplication, doing his best to play the innocent. "Can you honestly say that you feel nothing for me?"

Jane smirked. "Actually, right now I *feel* you just might be a better actor than Anthony Hopkins!"

He flinched at the sarcasm, actually taking a step back. "I thought you said all was forgiven."

"I did," she said. "But you have an uncanny capacity for committing multiple offenses in a single day."

"What have I done?"

"Never mind."

He sent her a doubtful stare. "I can only think that you're still feeling a little emotionally charged after all the hoopla lately. And in your condition—"

"Stop!" She thought she might explode if she heard one more word about her "condition." "You'd better go now," she said, pointing him toward the door. "My hormones are in overdrive already, and one more word along those lines from you just might have me reaching for heavy blunt objects."

Allan, looking alarmed, began backing toward the door. "All right, all right. But would you mind if I called you?"

She rolled her eyes, searching for patience. "Yes!"

"We could do something this weekend—" He saw her eyeing the metal doorstop at his feet and abruptly cut off his words. "Then again, maybe not."

When he was finally gone, Jane turned around and flopped into her desk chair, feeling as exhausted as if she'd just run a marathon. And no wonder. For the past weeks, she'd been on an emotional roller coaster whose dips and turns had left her breathless.

She felt something tickling her ear and started, fearing that Allan had somehow materialized in the room again. When she turned, however, she saw that it was only an iris from his bouquet. Allan's stand-in. The arrangement was really fantastically large and extravagant looking. Amazing really. And unforgettable. Just as Allan probably wanted it.

Why her? And why now? He had been able to forget her on their wedding day, but now, when he was practically a married man, he somehow couldn't leave her alone. She wondered when was the last time he had sent flowers to Patricia.

She glanced over at the bouquet again and grinned as a wicked little idea popped into her head. She picked up the phone and called a messenger service to come pick up a bouquet from Steele and Grimly and deliver it to Patricia Blakemore at WNYZ.

That done, she decided to get to work. And her first order of business, she decided, was to go through her Rolodex and decide which of Allan's clients would be the easiest and most profitable to steal away. After all, she had a child—Allan's child—to support. And hadn't he said that he wanted to help her in any way he could?

It was high time she started the long process of getting Allan out of her system, and one way to do that was to treat him as what he now was. A co-worker. Competition. Patricia's significant other. The second, and probably even more practical step she could take was to return her wedding dress. She would do that tomorrow morning. First thing.

Minutes later, she found the phone number for Mrs. Hoffman, a rich widow who she had always liked, and dialed.

Chapter Ten

Allan stood with his hand over the doorbell, wondering if calling on Jane was such a good idea. She'd made it pretty darn clear that she would rather have a swarm of bees on her doorstep than him. Still, he couldn't make himself go away, any more than he could have stopped himself from jumping in a cab and speeding to Brooklyn this morning to see her.

But he wasn't exactly relishing another resounding rejection from Jane, either, so he hesitated.

He just didn't get it. He was wildly attracted to her, they got along great—in those moments when she wasn't acting as if he had somehow offended her—and when they kissed, it was pure dynamite. He understood she might have some reservations about getting involved with someone new while she was pregnant, but he thought he'd been pretty open-minded about that, after the first moment of shock.

Okay, so maybe it had taken him a day to get back on an even keel. But he'd been fine by yesterday afternoon, and when he'd brought her the flowers he thought he might be getting somewhere. Then he'd asked her out, and she'd launched into her Linda Blair spinning-head routine.

Honestly, he just didn't get it. Was there something in his past that should have precluded his asking her out? Obviously, he'd been a workaholic, thick-headed jerk. But had he been such a jerk that she just didn't trust that he was a new person now? Maybe he had done something terrible. But why wouldn't he have heard about that?

It had surprised him a little when she said Grady didn't know about the pregnancy. When he'd talked to him, Grady had appeared to know what he was talking about. That was another puzzle. He couldn't quite figure out the Grady-Jane relationship, but he wondered if there weren't something more to it than he had previously thought.

Of course, he was never going to find the answers he was looking for if he just didn't go ahead and ring her buzzer. Maybe she wasn't even home. She might be out for a walk, or—

The guesswork was taken out of the question when the door flew open and she appeared, dressed in khakis and a loose sweater, and carrying a huge white clothes box. It looked like it might have held a coat, or an evening gown. When she saw him standing there her green eyes, which were tinged with dark circles, widened in surprise.

"Allan!"

He grinned. "I just happened to be in the neighborhood."

Her smile disappeared. "Allan, no one 'just happens' to come to Brooklyn, any more than anyone would just happen to go to Bulgaria. It's something you have to put a little thought into."

"Okay," he admitted, "so maybe I *thought* we could

take a walk. It's a beautiful Saturday, the birds are chirping, the smog has lifted....''

She laughed, then suddenly seemed to remember the box she was carrying. As if anyone could forget such a gigantic package!

He held out his good arm. ''Would you like me to help you with that?''

''No!'' She drew back.

What the heck did she have in there?

''Allan, what are you doing here?'' she asked, suddenly impatient.

''I came to forgive you.''

She looked at him with suspicion. ''Forgive *me?*'' she repeated. ''For what?''

''For sending your flowers to Patricia. You smoothed things over very nicely after the Brazilian restaurant incident.''

''That's good,'' Jane said with a sniff.

''No, that's terrible,'' Allan said. ''Just when I thought I might be very conveniently rid of her!''

Her eyes rounded with surprise and then focused so sharply on him that he suddenly felt like a bug under a microscope. A stinkbug, at that. ''What a terrible thing to say!'' she exclaimed in blustery indignation.

He laughed. ''But it's true. To hear her tell it, that cab ride with Grady nearly did her in. By the time they reached Columbus Circle, Grady had forgotten again that she wasn't you. They spent twenty blocks with him wedged in between the seats on bended knee, begging her to go to Westchester with him.''

Jane's lips turned up in a smile before she was able to catch herself. ''Really, Allan, you shouldn't have come all this way just to tell me that. Two minutes later and I wouldn't have been here anyway.''

"Then I arrived just in time," he said. "If you have somewhere to go, I'd be more than happy to escort you."

"That's not necessary. I know where I'm going."

"Wouldn't you like some company? I don't have a thing to do, so I can devote the entire day just to following you around."

Her expression told him that prospect was about as appealing to her as spending the day being tailed by a yapping poodle.

Given her less-than-thrilled reaction, he tried to keep his chin up, to remember their kisses. No one who kissed him like that could be so indifferent to him as she claimed. And if Grady was more serious about her than he had previously thought, Allan needed to move faster. "You can learn a lot about people from the errands they run, you know."

That seemed to absolutely panic her. "I don't want you snooping into my life," she said, holding onto the box so tightly that the cover bowed out. "You have no right—"

Her words cut off abruptly when she heard the squeal of brakes and belch of exhaust of a city bus trundling down the street.

"Oh, shoot, there's my bus!" Without further ado, she took off running.

Allan galloped after her, but he was amazed at how quick Jane was. Her long-legged sprint got her to the bus just in the nick of time, while he only managed to leap on, huffing and puffing, a split second before the doors closed.

He jumped up the three deep steps, intent on following Jane, when he was halted in his tracks by a bellowing reminder that nothing in life was free.

"Fare!" the bus driver barked.

All seven people on the sparsely populated bus looked up in alarm at the prospect of having a fare dodger in their midst. Allan, red-faced, took out his wallet and riffled through the bills there, looking for something small. All he had was twenties.

"Tokens or change," the driver snapped, and the bus, to Allan's surprise, lumbered forward again. Time and the Metropolitan Transit Authority apparently waited for no man, but what was going to happen if he couldn't come up with enough coins? Was he going to simply be tossed off?

In alarm he looked over at Jane, who was just seating herself halfway down the aisle. He gauged by her wicked little grin that seeing him tossed off was exactly what she was hoping for.

"*Correct* change," the driver said in disgust as Allan fumbled through a maddening number of pennies and nickels.

"Look, I can give you a ten," Allan said.

"Are you trying to bribe me, man?" the driver asked, offended.

Allan sighed at his rotten luck. He *would* have to run into a high-minded bus driver. "Yes, I am. Listen, I'm begging you. I'm desperate in fact. See that woman back there?"

The driver looked in the rearview mirror, and the rest of the passengers turned to stare at Jane, whose cheeks bloomed with color.

"I'm wild about her," Allan said. "And I had planned to spend the day with her, to let her know how much I—"

"Correct change," the driver said, cutting off his emotional declaration.

Allan was about to give up in despair when suddenly he heard the tinny sound of a token trickling through the coin receptacle. He glanced down in time to see an elderly lady in a crocheted sweater, a floral print skirt and Air Jordans snapping her pocketbook closed.

"Thank you, ma'am," Allan said.

She shook her head and smiled slyly. "You might not believe it, but young men used to chase me onto buses, too."

Allan laughed. "I believe it." He thanked her again and began to work his way down the unsteady aisle to Jane.

"You certainly handled that smoothly," she said.

"No obstacle is too great, no hurdle too high," he said grandly, plopping down in the seat next to her. "Now. Where are we going?"

"*I'm* going to Bay Ridge. You're getting off before then."

"Not a chance. Look how much trouble I had just getting on!"

She jumped up and held onto the grab bar running the length of the bus. "Then *I* will get off, and continue to jump on and off public transportation until I've lost you."

Allan frowned. "Say, it sounds as if you woke up on the wrong side of the bed this morning."

She let out a frustrated moan. "Allan, will nothing convince you to stop meddling in my life?"

At her words, he stood, too. "You act as if I've caused you some kind of trouble."

"Trouble is putting it mildly!"

"But I can't think of what I could have done."

"Everything!" she snapped. "Every time I'm ready

to get my life together, you appear and do something that throws me for a loop!''

"Like kissing you?" he asked.

"Yes!" she admitted, her face aflame. "Among other things."

Allan shook his head, trying to concentrate. "Does this have to do with something at the office?"

"No—I mean yes... Well, sort of." She sighed in frustration. "Allan, our entire lives were wrapped up in that office. Then it all became a snaggled mess."

"Then let's begin to unsnaggle," he said simply.

She looked at him squarely. "Some things can't be undone that easily," she admonished. "What about Patricia?"

Allan blinked. "You always insist on bringing Patricia into the mix, but honestly, Jane, when I'm with you I forget that she even exists."

She stared at him, horrified, as if he had just said he sometimes forgot about Christmas. "Don't you feel any responsibility for Patricia, and her situation?"

Allan shook his head. "Oh, in a nominal way, maybe. I guess I have put her in an odd position."

"Odd!" Jane exclaimed.

It was true, some part of him felt sorry for Patricia. In the pre-accident days, he had apparently spoiled her terribly. Maybe he'd even enjoyed the fake-sophisticated superficiality that she wore like a royal ermine mantle about her shoulders. It would be hard for her to absorb the fact that a man who had been pining away for her got a bump on the head and came to his senses and no longer worshiped the ground that her dainty size-six shoes walked on.

He shrugged. "Maybe it's time that Patricia learned to take her lumps."

Jane's mouth hung open in amazement.

"Look," Allan argued in his own defense, "I thought you of all people would agree with me. You have to admit, you're not too fond of the woman."

"But I don't want to see her treated so miserably!" Jane exclaimed. "And here I thought that you had turned over a new leaf, that you had changed. Come to find out, you're as tough and heartless as everyone used to say you were!"

He held his arm out in supplication. He even jutted his sling out toward her. "How can you say that? I'm full of heart—that's why I prefer you now to Patricia."

"And who will it be next month, or six months from now?" Jane asked him tartly. She wasn't moved by his words at all. In fact, the more he said he cared for her, the more offended she became. "I'll admit to having been fooled by you, Allan. You bamboozled me with your Mr. Charming act once or twice—but no more."

"There was no bamboozling intended," he argued.

He could nearly see the sharp retort poised on the tip of her tongue, but it was cut off when the bus lurched, sending the box under her arm flying. Allan reached out to grab it, but with his bad arm, he fumbled, and the box hit the ground, knocking it open. Suddenly, a voluminous white dress bedecked with tulle and pearls spilled into the aisle. A wedding dress.

Jane's wedding dress?

Allan reached down to pick it up, handling it gingerly, as though the material were spun of fragile glass. Here was another puzzle. What was Jane doing with a wedding dress? And why did it look as if she was returning it?

"Every time I'm ready to get my life together, you appear and do something that throws me for a loop...."

Her words echoed back to him, both in his mind and in the beet-red look of embarrassment on her face as she knelt next to him.

Slowly, he attempted to sort things out. "This is yours?"

After a long moment of hesitation, she nodded.

She hadn't wanted him to see it. Why?

Suddenly, a shocking possibility occurred to him. "Is this...were we..." He could hardly think of the words. "Were we going to get married at some point, Jane?"

She gaped at him, her expression so masked that he couldn't say whether he had hit upon the truth or not. As moments ticked by, however, and her look turned from surprise back to outrage, he feared that, far from hitting upon the truth, he had simply made another speculative blunder.

"What gave you that idea?"

"Well...the dress, for one thing. And you've been so adamant about not wanting to go out with me, I thought maybe that's what I had done to offend you."

"Ha!" she cried.

Ha?

It wasn't precisely an answer, but she snatched up the dress and stood, bristling with pride. "You *would* think that every woman in the world with a wedding dress wants to marry you, Allan."

He got up, too, feeling like an idiot. "So I guess I was way off base?"

"I don't want to discuss it."

"Then it's some other man you were going to marry—and I somehow interfered?"

"Yes, that's more like it," she said.

"Is the man you were going to marry the father of your child?"

"Well…" She hesitated for a moment, then blurted out, "As a matter of fact, yes."

Suddenly, Allan felt like a heel. All these weeks, he had been chasing zealously after Jane, never dreaming that somehow he was fouling up her life. She had tried to keep him at bay, to warn him off, but he had soldiered on as if it were some kind of game.

He would make it up to her. Somehow. He had to. He reached out and touched her arm. "I have to admit, Jane, I'm glad you didn't marry that other person, whoever he is. Call me selfish, but I really was going to give Patricia the heave-ho and try to put all my efforts into convincing you we would be good together."

She sucked in a shocked breath. "The *heave-ho?*"

"Well, yes," he admitted.

She pulled back from him, completely appalled.

"I would not only call you selfish, Allan," she said slowly, hurling each word toward him as if it were a little poisoned dart, "I would also call you incredibly egotistical! Good together? I've gone out of my way not to encourage you." She fairly shook with emotion. "And for your information, I *still* plan to get married, despite your interference!"

The words were like a bucket of ice water dousing him from head to toe. "But your wedding dress… I thought you were returning it."

"Well, I'm not," she said in a rush, adding, "I'm just getting it altered."

He couldn't believe it. He didn't want to believe it. But there was Jane…and there was her wedding dress…and here he was, feeling like a lunkhead.

His fingers held a white-knuckle grip on the bar. "So who's the groom?"

"It's…" She licked her lips, hesitating slightly before she tilted her chin and said, "Who else? Grady Grimly."

"YOU WANT TO *WHAT?*" Grady asked, amazed. He pulled Jane inside the lavish marble foyer of his apartment and shut the door.

"Marry you," Jane said.

He remained frozen, still in his silk smoking jacket and slippers at two p.m., staring at her, his brows raised suspiciously. "Why?" he asked, cocking his head like a puzzled bird.

"I thought you *wanted* to marry me," she said.

"I did—but you didn't want to."

"But now I do."

"Hmm." Grady thought for a moment. "I might need some time to think about this. Maybe discuss it with Dr. Winkel."

Jane prayed for forbearance. "Grady, I'm no psychologist, but I think I can clear this up for you. You asked me to marry you on several occasions, and now, after giving it some thought, I'm agreeing. You should be happy."

Grady remained frozen for a few long seconds, letting her words sink in. Finally, his eyes widened at the undeniable soundness in her logic. "By gum, you're right!"

"I know I am," she said, making a mental note that the first order of business after the marriage was to wean her husband away from Dr. Winkel. Poor Grady was so dependent on him that he didn't even see good fortune when it stared him the face.

Or maybe, she thought anxiously, he had good reason to doubt his fortune. After all, she had changed her mind for no better reason than she simply didn't want

Allan to presume that she was pining away for him. Wounded pride was not a good excuse for matrimony, except...

Except Allan was so intolerable, she hadn't been able to think of anything else to say!

And the more she thought about it—and she'd thought about it all morning—the more marriage to Grady would make sense. He would be a good father to her child...once she gathered up the nerve to tell him about the baby. Marriage and a family would be just what she needed to get her mind off Allan.

Miraculously, Grady's mood took a sudden shift from sullen suspicion to elation. "Wait right here," he commanded, then snapped his fingers. "Oh, shoot—I wanted this to be perfect. Come on inside anyway."

Confused, she nevertheless followed his instructions, walked into his spacious, sparsely furnished living room and sat down on the couch her new fiancé pointed to. All the furniture, modern in design, was beige or white, and the only splashes of color in the room came from the artwork on the walls, and pieces of sculpture standing out in the vast empty spaces.

She blinked in disbelief as she found herself staring at a Henry Moore figure in the corner of the room—a steel blob that was obviously supposed to be a woman—a piece that looked as if it had been heisted from the Museum of Modern Art's sculpture garden.

She waited in awed silence, wondering how long it would take to adjust to so much superfluous wealth, as Grady dashed to the other room and dashed back again, skidding to a halt in front of her. "Jane, will you marry me?" he asked.

"I just said I would."

"I know that, but say it again. I have a present for you."

"Oh, all right," she said, playing along. "I'd be happy to marry you, Grady."

He flipped open a tiny velvety square box, revealing the most stunning solitaire diamond Jane had ever laid eyes on. She gasped in the glow of its radiance.

"It's your engagement ring. Actually, I bought it as a last-ditch effort to convince you to marry me," Grady said. "You like it?"

She was stunned. The thing looked like something Elizabeth Taylor might wear. "I like it so much I promise I'll visit it at the bank vault every week."

He clucked his tongue. "Don't be silly. This was one of the more modest settings at Tiffany's. Besides, I read the other day that you can get little micro-alarms for your jewelry now."

"Alarm? You mean it goes off if someone tries to mug you?"

"Yes, like a car alarm. Isn't that great?"

Jane snickered. She could just imagine the thing going off—maybe in a grocery store if she and another customer were reaching for the same tomato.

"Don't laugh," he said. "I'll make an appointment to get you wired up ASAP. Tomorrow."

"Tomorrow's Sunday," she reminded him.

"Oh, sure, but they'll open for me."

Jane smiled at his sudden burst of self-confidence. "I don't see what the hurry is."

"Well we should go ahead and get it done, if you're going to be wearing the ring around town in the next week before the wedding."

"Week?" she asked. There was so much to do. And

she still hadn't told Grady about the small matter of her baby.

"Why, sure," Grady said, growing excited. "We can have it down at your father's farm—"

"What?" She couldn't imagine going back to her father's farm for a repeat performance of that disaster.

"You were going to marry Allan there," Grady pointed out, looking almost hurt.

"Yes, but that was Allan, and this…"

He puffed up in offense. "Well I know we don't have a snowball's chance in hell of booking Grace Church or St. John the Divine on short notice in April, and I don't want to wait. So doing it out of town would be the perfect solution, and that way we wouldn't have to invite throngs of people. Ceremonies like that are big money wasters."

As if she knew even half a throng to invite! "Okay, okay," she said, caving in. After all, he had just handed her a rock worth the gross domestic product of Belgium. The least she could do was marry him in Vermont. And a quick wedding would only help her situation, with the baby on the way.

Oh, how was she ever going to work up the nerve to tell Grady? She just couldn't do it now, when he was looking at her so expectantly, so hopefully. She wanted to start things out right between them, but if she told him about the baby, she feared things would never start out at all.

"I'll talk to Dad and see what he says."

At the mention of Will, Grady stared at her anxiously. "Does your father have to be there?"

"It *is* sort of traditional for the father of the bride to be present at these things, Grady."

He shrugged. "I just got the impression that he didn't like me very much."

"Don't be silly," Jane said. "Dad likes everybody."

Most everybody, she amended silently. But that most could be quite an exception...

"YOU'RE MARRYING *WHO?*"

"Grady Grimly, Dad."

"Good grief!" Will said over the phone with a long-suffering sigh. "How did this come about?"

"It's a long story, and I'm at work and can't talk now, but if you'll just tell me whether Saturday will be all right, and round up the usual suspects, I'll make all the arrangements with Reverend Woodwind...."

"So soon?"

"Daddy, you *wanted* me to get married."

"Well, sure, but first you were going to marry a bar-racuda, then when he got nice you decided you were gonna dump him, and now you've taken up with this Grimey fellow...."

"Grimly," Jane correctly.

"Same difference. Honey, are you sure?"

"Yes, Dad. Positive."

He sighed doubtfully, then said, "Well...I guess I can take the hundred-dollar cake out of the freezer and fire it up again."

Bad idea, Jane thought. Bad, bad, bad. Grady was already so prickly, the idea of having a half-eaten cake from her previously planned wedding might not sit too well with him. "Maybe we should get a new cake, Dad."

That suggestion was met with stony silence. When her father did speak, it was in the gravest tone. "Do you know how much that cake cost?"

She laughed. "A hundred dollars?"

"Darn tootin'!" he exclaimed. "What color hair does this fellow you're gonna marry have?"

"Dad, you *met* him. His hair's blond."

"Oh, right." He let out another long-suffering sigh. "I'll have to get another little plastic couple for the top of the cake, then."

Jane tried to think positively. The used cake might appeal to Grady's sense of economy. "I suppose we could patch over the eaten parts with icing."

"Sure, then turn them to the wall and nobody'll be able to tell a thing."

She screwed up her lips, then saw Allan rush past her office door, his face practically a thundercloud of temper. And there was something else different about him, too.

The sling was gone!

"Oh, Dad, I've got to go," she said, thanking him again before she crammed the phone back on its cradle. Then she trotted out after Allan, who snapped at the mailroom employee, Greg Stocker, standing out in the hallway.

"I guess he's feeling like his old self again," Greg muttered as Jane went by.

He certainly *looked* like his old self. Jane was puzzled.

Then an arm darted out from behind her and pulled her into a conference room. It was Grady.

"I did it!" he said.

"Did what?"

"I bought Allan out of his half of the business."

Her heart slammed against her ribs. "You did *what?*"

He shrugged. "I bought him out. It's part of my wedding present to you."

She stared at him, uncomprehending. "Allan's unemployment is a gift to me?"

He shook his head. "No, no, no. The business. Next month, we'll change the name from Steele and Grimly to Grimly and Grimly. It'll be the stuff those *Journal* features are made of."

Jane was appalled. She had never expected Grady to do anything like this! "Allan agreed to go?"

"Of course. I think he *wanted* to, actually. At least, he didn't put up much of a fuss when I confirmed that we were getting married. Now, did you talk to your father?"

She could hardly focus on the conversation she had just had with her dad, she was so stunned by this news about Allan. She wanted to go to him and assure him that Grady had acted on his own in this, without her input. The way things stood now, she felt as if she had double-crossed her old boss.

She remembered calling his old clients and blushed furiously. She *had* gone behind his back, but she never would have suggested buying him out of his business. Steele and Grimly just wouldn't be the same place without Allan. She already felt empty thinking about coming to work and his not being there. When would she ever see him?

But of course, that was part of the point. She shouldn't want to see Allan anymore.

"Jane?" Grady said, giving her a nudge. "What did your father say?"

"He said congratulations," she lied, still numb. "He'll be happy to have the wedding at the farm."

"Saturday?"

She nodded.

"Good," Grady said, rubbing his hands together. "Everything's falling into place nicely, don't you think?"

She couldn't stop thinking about Allan. "Will you excuse me?" she said, rushing for the door. "I'll check back with you in a minute."

She sped through the catacomblike hallways back to Allan's office. She didn't even bother to knock before entering.

Allan was reclining in his chair, his feet propped up on his desk. He looked sexier than she could ever remember seeing him; her heartbeat kicked into high gear just from glancing at him. He was hands-down the best-looking thing she'd ever laid eyes on.

Why couldn't she feel this way when she looked at Grady? she thought unhappily. Why was it only Allan made her feel this way—even when she was securely engaged to someone else?

"I didn't know," she said in a rush, coming to a stop directly in front of him.

He said nothing, but kept her pinned with his gaze.

She shifted uncomfortably from foot to foot as he slowly looked her up and down. "I swear, Allan, Grady just told me this minute, and if he'd asked my opinion on the matter, I never would have suggested—"

"I believe you," he said.

The dithering stream of words spilling out of her mouth stopped, and she looked at him curiously. "You do?"

"Of course."

She wasn't sure he did. "I was just worried that you might have thought that I had masterminded it all, first by stealing your clients—"

"You stole my clients?" His brows shot up. "Which ones?"

She reddened. "Well, Simington, of course. And I contacted Mrs. Smythe and Jack Leonard."

"The golfer?" She nodded reluctantly, but Allan merely laughed. "Sounds like something I might have done, back in the barracuda days."

"It was."

He sighed. "Well, far be it from me to hold that against you."

She shifted again. "Then you're not resentful?"

"Hell, no."

"Not even of being bought out of the business?"

"Especially not that!" he said, letting out a mirthless laugh. He stood up and began to pace, something else that reminded her of his old self. "To tell you the truth, I've been at sea here these past weeks. And Grady offered me so much money that I'll finally be able to start that ice cream business—and even have enough to fail spectacularly at it, which is a distinct possibility."

"You won't fail." She frowned, puzzled as he came to a standstill in front of her. "But if you're not mad about losing Steele and Grimly, or about me stealing your clients—why did you look so upset just now?"

"Can't you guess?"

She shook her head.

He looked at her squarely, with more emotion brimming in those gray eyes than she could ever remember seeing there, and admitted, "Because of you."

Jane was too surprised to breathe. Allan was losing his business—his baby, the thing he loved most in the world—and all he could think about was *her?*

"Once I leave here, I won't have an excuse to see

you anymore," he explained, "or to check up on how you're doing."

The words were so simple, so honest...so like how she felt herself.

Jane melted. Immediately and spontaneously, with virtually no resistance, she collapsed into Allan's arms and found herself engulfed in a kiss so passionate it took her breath away. She felt completely boneless and light-headed, almost as if all five foot eight of her had evaporated into thin air, and all that was left was the powerful attraction she felt for Allan deep down in her soul.

And her lips, of course. They were still there, moving against his in such a frenzy of need it felt almost as if they had melted together and were now one.

But Allan ran his hand down her back, across her hip, reminding her that her body indeed still existed— and wanted him something fierce. She shivered at his touch. For the first time since his accident, he was able to hold her in both of his arms, and she felt completely enthralled by the doubling of sensations as his newly freed arm skimmed up and down her spine, and then her arms.

She didn't know who moved first—they just seemed to shuffle as one toward Allan's desk. And then they were on it, shoving aside notepads and paper clips and pencil cups in a frenzy of arms and legs. She pulled Allan on top of her, longing to feel his whole length against her as she had once before.... Allan broke away from her lips but kept kissing her—her eyelids, her brow, her sensitive earlobes, which he nipped, causing her to let out a tiny cry and push her chest against him.

He looked down at her, feasting on her clothed body as if she were completely undressed before him. And then, with one hand he took both her hands in his, raising them above her head, and began to kiss his way down her jaw, and her arched neck, and...

And then Jane went off, detonating with a piercing wail that shook the walls.

Whooooooooop, whooooooooop, whooooooooop!

Her ring alarm! She had forgotten about it completely. Now it sounded like a car alarm going off inches from her ear.

In a panic, she pushed Allan, shot up to a sitting position and searched frantically for the little device in her suit pocket that turned off the alarm, but she was in such a sensual dither that it took her a moment to get her head on straight and remember exactly which pocket it was in. Footsteps thundered down the hall toward them.

"Hair!" she whispered frantically at Allan. She'd been running her hands through his hair, and now it looked as if he'd stuck his finger in a light plug. When that was taken care of, she hissed, "Lips!"

He wiped the lipstick off with the back of his cuff. Meanwhile, Jane was still frantically searching for the alarm controls when a group of curious employees appeared, huddling in the doorway.

Finally, Jane found the small plastic device in her right pocket and pressed the green button that had been demonstrated at the store. Blessed silence ensued. But when she looked up, everyone was staring at her. Including Grady.

"What happened?" he asked.

"I, uh, was congratulating Allan on the deal he'd made with you, and when we shook hands, the alarm went off," she said fumblingly. She prayed *her* lips weren't smudged, or worse, that the back of her skirt wasn't hiked up to her underwear. "I guess I'll have to be more careful."

Grady nodded, then trotted toward her. "Boy, that was great, though, wasn't it?" He marveled as he inspected the ring and the little black device in her hand. He was as excited as a little boy with a new train set. "Good and loud!"

"Yeah, that would be great on the subway," Allan agreed, with only the slightest hint of nervousness showing.

Jane, having made a quick tactile check of her backside and decided everything was okay there, managed a halfhearted chuckle herself, although inside she felt guilty. It was as if her conscience had shrunk into a tiny clot in the pit of her stomach. The rest of the employees dispersed, none of them having asked the obvious question that Grady was too absorbed in other things to ask: Why would she have been shaking Allan's hand with her *left* hand?

She looked at Grady, still innocently fiddling with her alarm controls, and felt about two inches tall. Next to him was Allan, looking twice as cool and collected as she felt, and showing about as much remorse as a seasoned Don Juan.

Life just seemed to get more and more confusing. How could she have promised to marry such a sweet man when she absolutely didn't love him? And how could she harbor such a strong desire for a man she absolutely shouldn't love?

Chapter Eleven

"Vermont!" Patricia cried in horror.

Allan nodded, smiling. He had thought about it all week. At first he'd considered going as far away as possible—to South America, or a tropical island somewhere. But something stopped him. Maybe it was that emptiness he'd been feeling since the accident. He had a hunch he wouldn't find the cause behind it by running away. And he feared he wouldn't be able to fill it without Jane.

"Have you lost your mind?" Patricia asked, though the tone of her voice left no doubt that she thought that he *had* gone insane. Nevertheless, she still looked confident that a little persuasion could set him straight again. "What's in Vermont?"

"It's where I intend to start my new business."

Two uneven lines puckered her brow. "Business?"

"The ice cream factory."

Her face fell. "Ice cream? You're going to try to make a business out of *that*?"

"Why not?" he asked.

"I can't think of anything more dismal, not to mention potentially bankrupting."

"To me it sounds like a lot of fun."

"Fun?" Her nose wrinkled in such strong distaste that at first Allan thought she was about to sneeze. "But darling," she cooed, "sometimes you have to think about the greater needs of society. Take my job, for instance. Certainly it may *look* like it's all fun and glamour, but still I know that I'm fulfilling a very important function in the world. Why, I'm practically a public servant. But making ice cream doesn't serve anyone except for the calorically foolish. Do you know I've gained two and a half pounds just from being around you these past weeks?"

Allan continued to smile. "So I take it you don't think much of my idea."

"Well, honestly," she went on, "I really couldn't jump on board any plan that required a move to Vermont, Allan. You couldn't possibly have forgotten what those bugs did to me out there! And there's not a thing to do. You don't want to spend the rest of your life eating hot dogs out in the middle of nowhere, do you? There aren't even very many people in Vermont—not ones worth knowing."

"I like Will."

Jane looked at him doubtfully. "The old man? Well, yes. He was a very rustic-type gentleman, and I'm sure he's very nice. But nice on a long-term basis is so dull!"

"It's a good thing you told me this before it was too late."

Patricia smiled and took a sip of the wine Allan had given her when she had arrived unexpectedly that evening. "I'd never forgive myself if I allowed you to follow some half-baked plan without warning you of the pitfalls."

Allan grinned back. Patricia was so full of misplaced

pride that he was growing almost fond of her. He'd never met anyone who took herself so seriously yet made herself so easy to laugh at. "Actually, I didn't mean that I was actually going to follow your advice."

Her mouth became a limp, ruby-red line. "You didn't?"

"No, I only meant that I'm glad you told me your feelings before I went to the trouble to ask you to visit Vermont on occasion."

He couldn't discern whether her blue eyes expressed shock over the fact that he wouldn't take her advice, or that he had only intended to invite her to Vermont "on occasion." "I can't believe it!" she said.

"Can't believe what?"

"That you would still go through with such a fool-hardy scheme." She licked her lips, desperately search-ing for another way to dissuade him. "What about Steele and Grimly? You can't just leave all that be-hind."

"But I already have."

She blinked. "What?"

"Grady bought me out. As far as Wall Street goes, I'm history."

Patricia recoiled. "Oh, Allan! You've got to do something. Tell Grady you made a terrible mistake. He knows you're not feeling well...." Her words trailed off, then she threw her hands out in exasperation. "But then, he probably knew that. I knew you couldn't trust that man. He's a walking disaster, throwing people into lakes, not to mention waiters!"

"It wasn't all Grady's doing, and I'm sure it wasn't a mistake."

"But to give up your job—"

He shrugged. "The factory will be a harder job than the office."

"Factory!" Patricia moaned. "Oh, Allan! It has such a, a—" she hunted for a word distasteful enough "—a *blue-collar* ring to it."

Allan beamed. "I can hardly wait to get started."

"Well!" Patricia said, darting up from the couch. "I can see we're heading in separate directions in our lives, Allan. You to Vermont, and me to my personal trainer."

He chuckled.

"I don't see how you can laugh about this. Don't you realize what you're giving up?" She gestured around his lackluster living room, which did have a bay window with a view of Central Park. "You won't find anything like this in Vermont."

"I won't miss it," he assured her.

"And then there's me."

He said nothing.

She crossed her arms, bristling. "Well don't think I'll change my mind, Allan. You'll never see me in Vermont, I can guarantee that!" She picked up her purse and marched to the door. "I can't believe what's happened to you, Allan. Didn't you talk any of this over with Grady?"

"I thought you said he couldn't be trusted."

"He can't, but that doesn't mean he's not a good friend. At least *Grady* would never give up Wall Street for the boondocks!"

"Grady's so busy now he'll hardly notice I'm gone. He's getting married to Jane."

"Thank heavens!" Patricia cried. "For a while I thought *you* were falling for that gangly mouse."

Allan had to bite back his anger. "I'm glad to know

what you really think of her," he said icily. "I was going to ask you to their wedding."

"Really?" she asked hopefully. The quickest way to Patricia's heart, apparently, was to invite her to a function. "When? Where?"

"Tomorrow. Vermont."

Patricia rolled her eyes, irritated with that plan—in fact, with the whole state. "Now how am I going to go there when I have to fly out to Boston tonight to do that segment on college admissions, which of course we have to do in Harvard Square. I can't exactly change all my plans for some little nobody's wedding. If fact, I don't even see why you're bothering to go."

He crossed his arms. "Grady's my partner and Jane's my friend."

She scoffed. "I think you're in love with her."

Allan gritted his teeth. "You'd better go now."

"All right, but don't expect me to come back," she warned, remembering her pride again now that she couldn't make it to the wedding. "I'm not going to waste my time with a Vermont-bound man, no matter how many bouquets of flowers you send this time."

She flitted out the door—probably expecting that he would run directly for the phone to dial FTD. Instead, Allan turned and walked back to the couch, relieved that she was gone. Now if he could just get himself out of Manhattan...and away from Jane.

Was Patricia right? Was he actually in love with Jane?

If so, he was in trouble. That alarm on her engagement ring had been more than an embarrassment. It had been a clear warning to him. She belonged to another man now. His old friend. He'd been wrong to attack her as he had.

But given the chance, he knew he'd do it again.

That was the terrible thing. He just couldn't imagine getting Jane out of his system. Jane said he had felt that way once about Patricia, too, so he had to take comfort from that fact. Now he could hardly care if Patricia was coming or going. Maybe in a while he would feel that way about Jane, too.

But he doubted it.

The doorbell rang, and he sighed. Apparently, he wasn't going to get rid of Patricia so easily after all.

He trudged to the door, wondering what more they could possibly have to say to each other, and flung it open, his lips set in a grim line.

But it wasn't Patricia at the door. It was Jane.

JANE CLEARED her throat. She had come here knowing exactly what she was going to say to Allan. She had a little speech all prepared, one she had practiced all week. But what she hadn't prepared for was seeing his face looking about as anxious to see her as a vinyl-siding salesman.

"I—I'm sorry," she stammered. "Is this a bad time?"

He shook his head as if to focus on precisely whom he was talking to, then he darted out his hand and grabbed her by the arm. "No!" he cried, adding softly, "don't leave."

But the electric shock that thrilled through her at his touch, not to mention the twinkle in his eyes, told her that she should leave. This wasn't going at all as planned. She had only wanted to come over and apologize for all that had happened, yet now she found herself being tugged, quite literally, toward his arms. She dug in her heels, keeping herself firmly planted in the hallway. "I can't come in. I'm in a terrible hurry."

"Have a date?"

She frowned, puzzled. "No."

"You mean Grady's left you all alone the night before your wedding?"

"Grady's working late tonight." She flushed when she realized how pathetic that probably sounded. "We're going to be in Martha's Vineyard all next week, you know."

He nodded, still watching her sharply. "On your honeymoon."

Honeymoon. He said the word in such a flat, toneless voice that she felt the anguish of it all the way down to her soul. She couldn't think about her wedding night right now. She had to concentrate on taking one thing at a time, and not get caught up in regrets. Like the regret that she wouldn't be honeymooning with Allan in Martha's Vineyard next week....

Stop it!

"Yes, our honeymoon," she said, her voice unexpectedly coming out just as flat as his had been.

"Well then," he said. "I suppose you're very busy tonight."

"Yes," she lied. All she really had to do was go home and pack. But with one practice run at marriage behind her, she didn't think filling a suitcase would take her very long. "Actually, I just wanted to dash by here to apologize."

At least, that was what she had told herself. Now she wondered. Could she have dropped by so she could look into Allan's eyes one last time? To convince herself she wasn't making a mistake?

"Apologize?" His brow furrowed. "What for?"

"For everything. For you losing your business—"

"I told you, that was my doing as much as Grady's."

"But it must look as if I elbowed you out, and I swear, that's not how it was."

"I know."

He said it with such assurance that she actually believed him. "Why don't you come inside?"

"I can't," she said quickly, knowing that was a bad idea just from the intensity of her desire to hurl herself across the threshold and into his arms.

"We can't just stand out here and talk," he said. "Don't you have time for a drink?" He gave her arm another little tug.

Although the added pressure as he squeezed her arm made her legs feel about as steady as wet noodles, she held her ground. "No, thank you. That's all I had to say."

"Really?" he asked. "When you said you wanted to apologize for 'everything,' I assumed there was more."

"Oh, well, there was," she admitted. This was awkward. "I also came to apologize for...kissing you on Monday."

The last two words were barely a whisper, but he apparently heard them loud and clear. A flame danced in his eyes, and he pulled her once more toward him. This time, she faltered a step before stopping herself. "You don't have to apologize for that," he assured her.

"But the alarm—"

"Believe me, I thoroughly enjoyed myself."

"But you shouldn't have. I'm engaged and you're..."

"In love with you," he finished for her.

She stood staring at him, frozen in time, feeling so

light-headed she feared she would faint. "You're what?"

His smile grew wider. "In love with you!" he repeated, almost joyfully now.

She still wasn't sure she had heard him correctly. Then he reached out, gathered her in his arms and carried her across the threshold. "Isn't that wonderful?"

Jane didn't know how to respond. For the first time in her life she had been literally swept off her feet. "Oh, Allan, you can't mean it—"

"But I do," he answered, giving her a twirl and kicking the door to his apartment closed. "I'm in love with you, Jane Fielding. Why won't you believe that?"

Why not, indeed?

For a long moment, she merely looked into Allan's eyes, letting his infectious glee melt away all her doubts. And finally, she *did* believe him. Allan loved her.

Like a delayed reaction to a physical shock, it struck her. *Allan loved her!* This was exactly what she had hoped for years and years. Of course, it had taken an ill-fated wedding, a clunk on the head, a few whopper lies and withholding the fact that she was having his child for him to reach this conclusion, but despite those minor details, she couldn't have been more elated. He loved her!

She smiled and threw her arms around him. "Oh, Allan," she said on a dreamy sigh.

He leaned forward, his lips inches from hers, then raised his eyebrows and asked, "Are you still wired?"

She barely noticed her ring flashing on her finger. Anyway, it didn't flash nearly as brightly as the spark in Allan's eyes. "Not at the moment, why?"

"Because I'm going to kiss you," he said, lowering his lips to hers.

This time, all that went off were the fireworks inside her own head as one sensation after another exploded inside her. She clasped her hands behind Allan's neck and drew herself even closer to him, reveling in the taste of his mouth, and the strength of his arms as he held her.

Jane gasped.

She forced herself to pull back, however much it pained her to drag her lips away from his. "Your arm!" she cried, struggling to wriggle out of his grasp.

"It's fine," he said.

"But we might hurt it again."

He cocked his head and grinned. "What did you have in mind?"

Just looking into his handsome face caused her insides to do double somersaults, and in that moment, she knew she was a goner. Again.

"Just this," she said, leaning forward to taste his lips once more.

He groaned with pleasure as he teased her tongue with his, and with that sound, Jane felt every other consideration slip away like an old terry robe being shucked off as she stepped into a steamy, pulsing shower. If Allan's arm hurt, he certainly didn't show it. And if guilt pricked her conscience, it was completely drowned out by the pounding of her blood.

All at once it seemed they were moving, spinning out of control, and before Jane could even surface for air, she felt herself being lowered onto the living room couch. She reached up and pulled him down on top of her, wanting to feel his weight against her.

Just like the other time, she thought vaguely as she

sought his mouth again. They became a tangled ball of arms and legs, but in the chaotic jumble of physical sensation, she felt an urgent question building in the back of her mind. Would Allan remember?

Would he remember the way their bodies fit together so perfectly, like two interlocking pieces of a well-oiled machine? They were perfect for each other. With no other man had she ever felt so at ease, so comfortable exploring the hard muscled power. Length to length, he felt just right, never making her aware of being too tall, or angular. Instead, her every curve seemed to match the contours of his own body, and he seemed to revel in the way she would wrap her long legs around him, anchoring him to her.

Would he remember how his every movement, touch and whisper brought out a corresponding response in her? If she stretched to nibble at his ear, he would send his hand skimming in a butterfly-light touch down to the soft swell of her breast, or her hip, or her thigh. When he dropped a playful kiss on her neck, she dug her fingers into the firm muscles of his shoulder blades, then ducked her head to find his lips again.

Most of all, she wondered if he would remember the wonderful emotional urgency as they began to tug at buttons and belts and zippers. It wasn't just physical release they sought so desperately, but a long pent-up explosion of desire, well-hidden passion for each other and love.

He'd said he loved her. Last time, she had said she loved him.

Even now, she was aware of the slightest swell in her abdomen. He had fathered the delicate life inside her. Their baby. Would he notice that, too?

Would he remember?

It suddenly seemed as if all life's possibilities were opening up to her. Allan would remember. They would be happy together, just as they were in this moment, forever.

Jane gasped as Allan teased one breast with his hand, and all her thoughts took a back seat as more immediate, frustrating problems loomed larger…like how to get her shirt off without letting go of Allan. Try as they might, they both finally had to bow to the laws of physics and separate only for the few moments it took to discard their remaining clothing.

And when they found each other again, this time with bare skin against bare skin, it felt even more explosive. She saw a flame in Allan's eyes where before there had only been a spark, and when he traced the silhouette of her entire form, she felt the heat down to her very soul.

Impatiently, she pressed against him, longing to feel him inside her again, to relive herself the abandon he had shown her once before. She ran her hands up and down his arms, relearning their corded musculature. She endowed every teasing, exploring movement with a kinesthetic reminder. *Remember this touch*, was the meaning her fingertips tried to convey. And when she kissed him hungrily, it was as if to say, *Remember this, Allan? Remember the intimacy we shared once before…?*

Her sudden burst of unbridled desire surprised him. He ran his hands through her hair then cradled her head by the temples as he looked down into her eyes, his own gaze full of wonder.

"I love you, Jane," he repeated softly.

"Oh, Allan, I—"

He stopped her by dropping a light kiss to her lips. "You don't have to say a word," he said. "Just let me love you."

That was fine with her. In fact, it was what she wanted right now more than anything else in the world. Just hearing him say the words she so longed to hear released a tide of passion in her so strong that she felt she might die if she didn't kiss him again immediately.

As she felt all of him against her, the hardness of his male length pressing insistently against the most intimate part of her, it was impossible for her not to remember the time before. Though they had both been a bit tipsy, their lovemaking had been nothing as unstructured as this. They had at least made it to her bed. And while the images of that night were a blur, a few things still stood out in her mind: Her first long look at Allan undressed, looking more magnificent than her fantasies had ever imagined. Her telling him she loved him. And this—this feeling of being completely engulfed by another person, as though she were about to drown in her own need.

Allan was her life raft, and she held on to him for dear life, clinging to his arms, his back, his shoulders, arching against him while he stroked the core of her womanhood, moving against him as if she just couldn't get close enough. And as the heat built inside her, she couldn't. She wanted him inside her, desperately, as if feeling him filling her would breach the turbulent sea of half truths, lies and fictions that had stood between them all these weeks.

Exactly when she felt she could stand no more, Allan knelt between her legs and thrust himself inside her. She gasped, unprepared for the frenzy of desire he unleashed within her. He moved inside her patiently, straining to take it slow, his every movement a sweet agony. Especially when she looked into his eyes and saw the barely leashed control there. And the vulnerability.

Even at the height of passion, the old Allan had never let her see his weakness, his desire, his fear. He had kept himself guarded. But now it was as if Allan were laying his soul open to her, giving all of himself.

She trembled with the effort of doing what he asked, of just letting him love her. Ultimately, she failed. "Oh, Allan," she said, her voice breathless and husky, "I love you so much."

He stilled for a moment, staring down at her in almost reverential wonder, and then completely lost control. Jane gave herself to him with such zealous abandon that it felt as though she were reeling. They moved against each other in a frenzy of need, punctuated with soft moans and whispered endearments that made her smile even as she lost herself in the firestorm of their release.

And when finally she hugged Allan against her, his body pliant and spent, her smile continued on as a feeling of deep contentment spread through her. Yes, she was lying in the arms of one man on the eve of her marriage to another. And yes, she still had quite a few secrets—including a child—that she was keeping from Allan. Yes, her life was now a complete, tangled mess—but it finally all seemed fixable.

Allan loved her. Somehow, this was all going to work out.

After a few minutes, he slowly rolled to one side, cradling her loosely with one arm. She turned to snuggle against him, but was stopped cold by the somber expression on his face.

"Is anything wrong?" she asked.

He turned to her. "Why?"

"You looked so…" She shrugged, feeling a ripple of anxiety dance up her spine. "I thought maybe I had hurt your arm."

"No..."

The way he voiced that one simple word spoke volumes. It wasn't his arm that was stinging, but something else.

What? Was he thinking about Grady? Patricia?

Jane felt herself blush suddenly as the memory of those two individuals came slamming back into the forefront of her consciousness. Oh, dear! How was she going to explain this to Grady? How could she make him understand?

And Patricia... Well, of course she had a great deal less sympathy for her. After all, Patricia had had Allan's love in the palm of her hand all along, and then tossed it casually to the winds to run off with someone else. And yet, Patricia was also in the same boat that Jane was in....

And Allan would always be the father of both their babies.

But right now he only knew Patricia was pregnant, so of course he would be worried about her, and feel a certain amount of guilt. Lucky thing she thought of that before she might have stupidly decided to blurt out the news of her own condition. Right now, Allan looked as if he were in need of assurance.

She reached out to gently touch a hank of hair that had fallen over his forehead, and he flinched. Jane stiffened. "Something *is* wrong," she said.

He looked distracted, and shook his head. "It's nothing. Just..."

His words trailed off, but Jane could easily have filled in the blank. *Just that he felt he had made a terrible mistake.*

She brought her hand back to her side. As the glow of love inevitably began to fade from her cheeks, it was replaced by a startling blush of realization. Perhaps she had been mistaken, too. For the truth was, making love had apparently rung no bells inside Allan's head. He didn't remember that they had made love before.

He didn't remember.

Her breath began to come in short, labored gasps. How could he not remember? Hadn't their lovemaking meant anything to him? She wondered whether she had been mistaken to believe him when he told her he loved her. Allan wouldn't be the first man to tell a woman a lie to get her into the sack.

Or onto the couch.

By the time the phone rang, her face was flaming.

Allan, carefully extricating himself from their cold love nest, sat up and reached for the cordless phone on the end table next to the couch. "Hello," he said. In the moment that followed, he glanced aside to see whether Jane was watching him, which of course she was. He might be a rat twice over, but he was a rat with a gorgeous body that she couldn't take her eyes off. "Oh, hi," he said.

Though his voice tried to hide it, she knew. It was Patricia.

"There's no need to apologize," he told her tightly. Had they just had a fight? "No, never mind that now." He rolled his eyes.

Jane felt her hot cheeks grow hotter with every word that came out of his mouth. Apparently, she had stepped right into the middle of a hornet's nest, and provided the hornet with a perfect way to get even with Patricia.

Oh, how could she have been so foolish—twice!

As Allan continued to argue with Patricia, Jane began to scoop up her clothes and put them on as quickly as possible. It didn't matter if buttons and buttonholes didn't quite match up, or even that her panties were on inside out. She needed to get out of there!

Allan sighed impatiently into the receiver. "Look, can we talk about the wedding later?"

Jane winced. Wedding? He had never told her about any plans he and Patricia had made.

No kidding! she scolded herself. For weeks Allan had been trying to seduce her. A man didn't usually fess up to being engaged to one woman when he was trying to have a fling with another.

A fling. She shook her head as she shoved her foot into a low pump. How could a mere fling have seemed so emotionally and physically earth-shattering to her? Of course, she wasn't exactly experienced in matters of the heart—or the flesh, for that matter—but Allan had seemed so in sync with her.

He had told her he loved her, even. Had he lied?

The thought made her feel weak, almost physically ill.

Allan suddenly glanced over and saw her advanced stage of dress. "Look," he told Patricia, "I'll call you later."

Jane waved her hands frantically, trying to tell him not to get off the phone on her account.

"I've got to go now," he said. "No, nobody's here."

At that, Jane almost snapped. She lurched away from the couch in search of her purse, which she must have dropped somewhere near the doorway.

"Goodbye," Allan said, hanging up the phone. He rushed over, heedless of the fact that he wasn't wearing a stitch of clothing, just as Jane was reaching for her pocketbook. He grabbed it by the strap and held on as if it were a rein to stop her. "Where are you going?" he asked, frazzled.

"Home." She tried to avert her eyes from his naked form, but failed.

"You can't," he said. "We need to talk. I feel so confused...."

He had that plaintive look again. Jane felt a melting reaction to the attraction of those gray eyes, but she fought against it—especially when she considered what their "talk" would be about. Whatever he might genuinely feel for her, he obviously still felt more for Patricia.

"I have work to do," she reminded him. "I'm getting married tomorrow, remember?"

His hands held her purse in a white-knuckle grip, and his gaze turned icy. "No, you're not."

The nerve! Did he think he could give her orders just because she had succumbed to him in a moment of weakness? "You're not my boss anymore, Allan."

"I know that," he said. "I'm your lover."

And soon, apparently, he hoped she would be his mistress. What was she supposed to do, play second fiddle to Patricia for the rest of her life?

The strange thing was, not a month ago she had been willing to settle for that. She had been willing to take Allan on whatever terms he offered, including a marriage of convenience. But not now. If she couldn't have his love, completely and exclusively, she didn't want him, period. She would be better off marrying Grady and forgetting all about Allan. All about love.

"I've got to go," she said, turned to open the door. But she still found herself caught by her purse strap. She tugged on it to no avail. "Do you play tug-of-war with everyone at your house, or is it just me?"

"I can't let you go," he said. "Not without talking about what just happened."

She released a tired breath. "What just happened was a mistake, Allan, and you know it."

"No," he said. His face took on that confused expression again. "You said you loved me...."

Jane blushed, then defended herself in the only way she could think of. "I lied. I didn't mean it."

He reacted as if she had just delivered a stinging slap to his face. "Lied?"

She shrugged guiltily. "In the heat of passion, people are likely to say anything...."

Hadn't he?

"I've always heard they're more likely to speak the truth."

Jane felt like stamping her foot in frustration. Why didn't he just drop it? Was he just trying to humiliate her? "Look, Allan, what we just did was terrible. Grady is your friend...my fiancé. I have several very good reasons for marrying him."

Allan's eyebrows shot up. "But not love?"

She couldn't answer. "Goodbye, Allan," she said, pulling on her purse with all her might.

"Just wait and let me put on some clothes," he said. "Just let me walk you to the street at least."

"No, I have to go now!"

Finally, Allan let go of her purse, and the release of pressure nearly sent her reeling back across the threshold.

"We're not through," he told her.

"Yes, we are," she said definitely, then turned and fled, before he could get dressed and catch up with her.

And this time, as she stumbled down the hall toward the elevator, she felt she had spoken the truth. The emphatic, unchangeable truth. She was going to marry Grady tomorrow, and that would be the end of her and Allan.

Chapter Twelve

"She won't talk to you, Allan."

Allan swore under his breath. He knew it wasn't kosher to curse over the phone to the man he was hoping to have as a father-in-law, but he couldn't help it. "I've just got to talk to her, Will."

"She won't come to the phone."

"She wouldn't talk to me when I tried to call her last night, either."

"I'm surprised she even picked up the phone."

"She didn't. I meant when I called up to her from the street," Allan corrected. "She didn't even stick her head out the window to tell me to get lost."

"Well, if it's any consolation to you, son, she arrived here on the first train this morning looking like something thawed out and warmed over. You must have at least made her lose some sleep."

"I love her, Will."

"Did you tell her that?"

"Of course I told her. And I sang it into her answering machine. I even serenaded it to her on a Brooklyn street."

He could imagine Will's perplexed expression—it probably wasn't too different from his own. Why in the world was Jane being so stubborn? After yesterday, Allan knew that she didn't love Grady. No woman could lose herself in his arms one day then turn around and marry another man.

Could she?

She said she loved *him*. Allan. And those words had stirred such a firestorm in him, such an odd unsettling confusion, that he had muffed everything. But why had her bold confession of love been so startling? *"I love you, Allan."* Even now, the memory of those words caused his temples to throb.

Why would she marry Grady when she loved someone else?

Maybe she thought she was providing her child with a stable home, but Allan knew now that it took more than a man in the house to constitute a happy family. It took a real father, something he'd never had. Something he was prepared to be for Jane's baby, no matter who its father was. He would be there for his or her first step. Then, if it was a boy—heck, even if it was a girl—he would take him fishing, or to Little League practice. Girls these days could be pretty tough. And any girl with Jane for a mom was bound to be just as driven and single-minded as she was.

But no matter what sex the child was, he hoped that he and Jane could raise it with so much love that it would never lose sight of the important things in life. Love and security. Or lose interest in the frivolities that made life so unique. Ice cream. Music. Or forget that love can almost always be found in the people nearest you, whom too often we take for granted. Jane. What had he been thinking all those years, working alongside her but letting her get away from him?

"Allan, you still there?"

Allan gritted his teeth. "Yes, but not for long." Jane might be stubborn, but she would find that he could be pretty determined himself. When faced with the prospect of losing Jane, he could still be as much of a barracuda as ever. "I'm on my way."

"Hallelujah!" Will cried. "But I should warn you. I don't know what your chances are going to be."

"It's even money, Will. Are you aware you've got the most stubborn daughter in the world?"

"Sure am," Will said, and added doubtfully, "and if she's decided to marry this grim groom of hers, I'm afraid there's not much either of us can do to stop her."

For the first time this morning, Allan cracked a smile. "Oh, isn't there?"

ONE MORE BAR of "Our Love Is Here to Stay" and Jane felt she might rocket right through her father's kitchen ceiling in a bride-white fireball.

"Dad, can you please go ask Aunt Katherine *not* to sing that song?" Jane asked Will as she strode, nervous as a cat, across the kitchen in her wedding dress, veil fluttering anxiously behind her.

Her father shrugged. "She's got to warm up, honey."

"No, I meant…well, do we really need music at this thing, anyway?" Jane asked, blanching when she realized that she had just referred to her marriage ceremony as "a thing," as if it were a fifties horror movie.

Deep down, she knew what she was doing was right. Grady would be a stabilizing force in her life, a father for her child—whenever she got the nerve to tell him there was going to be a child. She was just so afraid of losing Grady if she told him the truth. Because, most important, marrying Grady was a way for her to get Allan out of her mind once and for all. The only trouble was, the closer she came to the moment to say "I do," the less appealing that moment became.

"Well, Janie," her father explained, "you said to round up the usual suspects for this little affair, and that's what I did. And I suppose the suspects have rounded up their usual songs. You don't want to hurt anyone's feelings, do you?"

"No, but—"

"What do you think?" He gestured with pride to his cobbled-up cake. As promised, the eaten sections had been covered with white icing, and atop the third tier stood a brunette bride and a blond groom.

"Very nice," Jane said. It still looked like a wedding cake with some hunks taken out of it, but that was beside the point. Frankly, she was surprised that her father seemed so caught up in details.

He raised his eyebrows, sending a slew of deep creases across his forehead. "You shouldn't even be down here, should you?"

She shrugged, reaching over without thinking and skimming off a piece of icing from along the bottom of the cake. "Why not?"

Her father slapped her hand away from the cake. "Bad luck," he said. "Grady might come in and see you."

"That *would* be terrible." She couldn't imagine doing anything that could heap more bad luck upon her than what she had done already. Surely sleeping with another man the day before her wedding was tempting the fates more than traipsing around the wrong room in her wedding dress.

Her father patted her on the back. "Perk up, Janie. This is your wedding day."

She straightened a little, and though it was difficult

in a dress that felt like a vise against her rib cage, managed a half smile. "Do I look so bad?"

"Like a bride in need of Prozac." He frowned. "Something's really wrong, isn't it?"

She shrugged.

Will sighed and said, "Well, I guess if I really wanted to know what was going on I should have asked Allan when I spoke to him this morning."

"How long did you talk to him?" she asked.

"Oh, a while..." her father answered. There was something teasingly provocative in the way his voice trailed off.

"What did he say?"

"I thought you didn't want to hear from him ever again."

"I don't. I just want to know what he said to *you*."

He looked at her warily. "Now, Janie, this was a private conversation."

Private. That sounded suspiciously as though they were talking about her. "Is Allan coming to the wedding?"

Her father stared at her, not giving an inch. "I thought the bride was only supposed to have eyes for her groom."

Jane looked from a rolling pin left lying on the counter to her father's cake, then back again. To get the information she wanted, she actually debated threatening the life of the hundred-dollar cake—what remained of it.

And then Grady came scuttling in. First he looked at the cake, then at Jane in her wedding dress. Behind their glasses his eyes became as wide as saucers, though he covered them as soon as possible with his hands.

"What are you doing in here!" he cried.

"Talking to Dad," Jane said simply.

"Well, shouldn't you do that in a bedroom or something? I can see you!"

"Even with your hands over your eyes?" Will wondered.

"No!" Grady cried. "But I *saw* her—"

"Then we've already got bad luck working against us," Jane said. "So you might as well take your hands away from your face."

Grady did, but he still looked annoyed. He also looked surprisingly handsome in his morning coat and striped trousers—just like an old-fashioned bridegroom. But his good looks didn't send the same kind of thrill through her that she got just by looking at Allan. And somehow, not finding her groom-to-be pulse-racingly handsome made her feel guilty all over again.

"Good heavens, Jane," he said. "You're cursing our marriage."

Jane didn't have the nerve to tell him that their marriage was probably already cursed. "You can't really believe in those superstitions," she said.

"Why not?" he asked. "Dr. Winkel told me I should be very careful marrying you."

Then Dr. Winkel was wiser than Jane had always assumed. The man was bound to know that no woman would put up with being second fiddle in her husband's life to a psychologist. Although he might have other reasons for warning Grady against her. "He probably thinks that I'm out to steal your money."

"That too," Grady admitted readily. "But mostly it's just that he believes in going by the book, traditionwise. He even wrote an article about it once. Something about rituals being anchors or foundations..." Grady thought for a moment, then lifted his shoulders. "Oh, I don't know. I should let him speak to you about it all, but I guess now is too late.''

"Is Dr. Winkel *here?*" Jane asked.

"Of course," Grady said. "He's my only guest. Well, the only one who's arrived yet."

At her first opportunity to meet the illustrious man of the mind, Jane temporarily forgot her other problems, rushed to the kitchen door and looked through the crack to try to make out the guests milling around in the living room. There were relatives and her father's neighbors, and even Dr. McGillicutty had shown up. Jane finally spotted a short man with a natty goatee—he *had* to be Dr. Winkel—but the person who really caught her eye was the woman standing next to him.

"Patricia Blakemore's here!" Jane exclaimed in surprise.

Grady nodded, looking over her shoulder to see out, too. Patricia was standing alone in the center of the room, sipping at champagne. "Of course. But she's not what I would call my guest."

"Who invited her?"

"She said she was waiting for Allan. She just drove in from Boston."

Jane shot a questioning glance at her father. "Is Allan coming here?"

"Why not?" her father asked.

So he *was* coming. Most likely, that was what he had been telling Will on the phone this morning. But he was probably only coming to meet Patricia.

What did she expect? That Allan was going to ride up on his trusted steed at the last minute, profess eternal love and rescue her from marrying the wrong man?

Grady wasn't the wrong man, she repeated to herself. For her purposes, he was the only man. Allan would have been the wrong man, because he was bound to Patricia, whom he had always loved. Patricia, who was going to have his baby.

The blood in Jane's veins turned to ice water and she stared out at Patricia once again.

Patricia, who was swilling champagne as if it were going out of style!

Acting on pure gut instinct, Jane bolted out the door before Grady could grab the back of her dress. She made her way across the living room, ignoring the gaping stares of her relatives, who were no doubt wondering what was going to go wrong this time.

She strode right over to Patricia and grabbed the stem of her champagne flute as it was halfway to her lips. "Please, Patricia, don't!"

She might have stopped the movement of the stemware, but unfortunately, the fluid just kept moving—splashing a surprised Patricia square in the face.

Patricia exclaimed and jumped back, twitching to shake the champagne off her face and hair and wiping it out of her eyes with one hand. "Are you crazy?" she asked Jane, making a sour face. "I'm all wet!"

"I'm sorry, but you shouldn't be drinking right now, Patricia," Jane told her earnestly, reaching over to grab a napkin from a side table and handing it to the newswoman. "It's such a critical time."

Patricia stared at her as if she had grown two heads. "Am I supposed to stay sober because you're getting married?"

Jane shook her head. How pathetic! Was the woman so vain that she would deny the truth to the detriment of her own child? "I'm talking about the baby, Patricia."

She continued to gape at her. "What baby?"

Jane suddenly felt a prick of discomfort. "Well… yours."

"I'm not having a baby!" Patricia said.

"You're not?"

"No!" the woman exclaimed, then narrowed her eyes and asked, "Where did you hear this rumor? Liz Smith?"

"No…" Jane knew Patricia would be disappointed if she discovered the source of the rumor was someone as lowly as Grady.

"Why would anyone think I would have a baby right now—now, when I'm finally getting somewhere at the network?" Patricia asked. "My goodness! Don't you realize a baby would ruin my image as a New York sophisticate?"

"Oh…well, I guess." Jane was so confused. If Allan and Patricia *weren't* having a baby, then all the time she had been thinking Allan was being so callous toward his old girlfriend, he had probably just been speaking the truth.

Did Allan really not love Patricia?

Had she misunderstood their phone call yesterday?

Jane felt someone tapping her on the shoulder. It was Reverend Woodwind. "I think we really should get started, Jane. It's already past eleven. And at twelve…"

At twelve he had another golf game. The man should give up the cloth for the PGA, Jane thought in annoyance. How could she get married now, not knowing what Allan really felt about Patricia—and herself? Had he really meant it when he said he loved her?

"We need to wait for Allan," Jane said hurriedly. "We can't have the wedding without him."

Patricia smiled. "I'll fill him in on every little thing he misses," she promised.

Grady was tugging her up to the front of the room. Suddenly, just as before, Aunt Katherine came bustling in with her sheet music and made a beeline for the piano. The guests closed ranks in back of the wedding party. Jane felt her leg muscles turning to Jell-O, and yet her father was suddenly right next to her, holding her up. He, too, looked anxiously around the room.

"Allan's not here?" he asked.

"Don't worry," Grady, on the other side of her, said with some impatience in his tone. "He'll be here."

But when? Jane thought. And how was she going to delay the wedding until then?

But it turned out she didn't have to. As she stood, heartbeat fluttering when Reverend Woodwind cleared his throat, she felt something on the other side of her give. She looked down in horror to see her father on the ground, clutching his chest.

"Dad!" Jane collapsed to the floor next to him. "Someone call a doctor! Fast!"

PAST ELEVEN! Allan needed to find the Fielding farm, fast. He just couldn't consider the possibility that he wouldn't make it in time to stop the wedding. Hopefully, Will was doing his part.

He looked over at the directions he'd gotten from Will just that morning, which he'd scribbled hurriedly on a napkin. They weren't very precise, and he was having a hard time following the obscure landmarks. Like the next one. "Turn right at dirt road." As if there were only one! He felt as if he had passed a million— and at a speed that would have made Mario Andretti envious.

He hugged a curve and tried to concentrate on finding the right dirt road—or a little bridge that he was supposed to have hit earlier. He had thought he'd gone over one, but now he was seeing little bridges everywhere and feared he might have made a mistake somewhere along the way.

He felt so hot and clammy with nerves that he rolled down the window, and the ensuing gust of air sent his napkin-map flying down to the floor. He reached over to get it, feeling a strange sense of déjà vu as he bent toward the passenger side floor mat. He had driven this road before. In a hurry. Lost.

Late for a wedding!

The same strong sting of confusion he'd felt when Jane told him she loved him struck him once again. Wedding... Jane loved him.... Something about all this was adding up.

At the sudden shiver that went down his spine, he straightened up again, having just barely managed to grab the napkin. But it was too late. To his horror, he saw a black-and-white splotched cow step out into the road.

Zelda!

Will's only remaining darling stared at Allan with wide brown eyes. Running on pure adrenalin, Allan hit the brakes and started turning the steering wheel like mad, doing anything he could to avoid hitting Zelda.

The car screeched and spun, spitting loose gravel, dirt and then grass as it was tossed into a culvert. Allan had the vehicle almost under control, and might have gone on unscathed, if it just weren't for that darn phone pole, which brought the car to an abrupt, jarring stop that turned explosive when the air burst out of the air bag in a split second.

For a few moments, Allan sat behind the wheel, still gripping it as if he were moving at full speed, stunned from the impact. The air bag had receded into a flaccid lump in front of him, and he did a quick visual check to make sure he was all in one piece. He was, of course, which meant that there was nothing else to do but pull the car out of the ditch and hunt down that damn farm.

He put the car into reverse and then froze.

That *damn* farm?

Will's place was one of the most heavenly spots on earth. What the heck was the matter with him? He loved Vermont.

Vermont! Finally, it struck him. The déjà vu, his cranky mood…the wedding!

A flood of memories came rushing back to him. Like a man whose life passes before his eyes before he dies, his own passed before him now, though his own had just been saved. But the images were confusing. It was his own wedding he was going to, not Grady's…wasn't it?

Slowly, understanding dawned. His wedding to Jane…that had been a few weeks ago.

He had begun feeling a strange sensation yesterday, when he was making love to Jane, and she told him that she loved him. As though she had told him that before, as though they had made love before. And now he knew.

They had. They were going to be married. But then he'd been in a wreck, and had been struck with amnesia, and now Jane was going to marry Grady.

Quicker than he could say "dearly beloved," Allan was back on the road, racing frantically toward what he assumed must be the entrance to Will's farm. He had to stop that wedding, to tell Jane he understood everything now, and let her know that he was back to his old self.

That horrifying thought brought him to another screeching stop. His old self? Oh, no!

Allan tried to think of a joke, but was too nervous. Then he tried to think of his favorite ice cream. Boysenberry walnut. That was a good sign. Finally, he turned to the newspaper folded in the seat next to him and hunted down the business page in search of the NASDAQ trading figures. When he found them, he felt no emotion, no speeding of his heartbeat, no fluttering of his pulse.

He breathed a sigh of relief. Maybe he wasn't completely back to his old self, after all. Now if he could just get to Jane in time to convince her that he was ready to give her the best of both Allans!

JANE WAS SO WORRIED about her father that she just couldn't keep her mind on the minister's words. Dr. McGillicutty had examined her father and pronounced Will perfectly able to sit quietly through a marriage ceremony. Unfortunately, Will wasn't sitting quietly. He was fidgeting, moaning and coughing spasmodically.

Twice Jane had stopped the minister so she could run over and check on Will herself. Twice, he had refused to call an ambulance. He let out a wheezing sigh and Jane considered stopping the ceremony for a third time, but the last time she had dashed over to the couch, her father had asked her if she might not be using her apparent worry about his health as a way to avoid marrying Grady.

Was she that easy to read? Jane wondered. For now, as she stood in front of the minister, her sweaty hand clutching Grady's disturbingly dry one, she knew she didn't want to marry him. The hitch was, she wasn't certain when exactly she could bring up the fact that she had changed her mind. At this point, there weren't many inconspicuous moments left.

What had she been thinking, promising to marry Grady? It was obvious to her now that she could never marry a man she didn't love. And she *had* loved Allan for all these years, even these past few weeks, no matter how angry she had been with him.

Jane felt frozen, dazed, when suddenly out of the fog she heard the minister's voice announce, "…speak now or forever hold your peace."

Not hesitating, she lifted her bouquet in the air like the only student in class who knew the answer to the teacher's question. "I can show just cause," she said, creating a wave of gasps from behind her—not to mention from Grady beside her.

"Jane, have you lost your mind?"

She turned to Grady. "I'm sorry, Grady. I should have told you before. I'm pregnant."

There was nothing but silence this time, and an utterly horrified look from Grady, who recoiled from her as if she'd just asked him to give her his life savings. "What?"

"I'm pregnant," she repeated. She turned to Will, who had jumped up from the couch and was suddenly well enough to have sprinted to her side. "I'm sorry, Dad—I should have told you, too."

He didn't look the least bit pained by her bombshell. "That's all right, sweetheart."

Suddenly, the front door burst open and a frazzled Allan came bursting through, arms flailing. "Wait!" he cried. "Stop the ceremony!"

Jane looked at him, beaming. *He came!* Maybe he hadn't galloped up on a great white steed to steal her away, but he had made it somehow. She ran over to him.

"I already did," she said.

"You mean you aren't going to marry Grady?"

She shook her head.

"Listen," he told her in a rush. "I just had another accident with Zelda."

Jane grabbed his arm. "Are you all right?"

He nodded. "Jane, I understand everything now—well, almost everything. My amnesia's gone. I know we were about to be married. Why didn't you tell me?"

"Because you were driving the other way when you had your wreck."

He frowned. "All I remember is that right before the accident I remembered you telling me that you loved me. Maybe it took a bump on the noggin to appreciate what a gift that was."

Jane sent an anguished glance toward a stunned Patricia, Grady and all the disapproving guests who were closing in on them. "Oh, but, Allan, I've messed things up so much!"

He grabbed her by the forearms. "Not irreparably," he told her. "I'll make things right. And when you have your baby, I'll love it like it was my very own. In fact, it *will* be my own, because I intend to marry you, Jane Fielding."

Jane couldn't help the smile that seemed to radiate from every pore in her body. "It would have been yours in any case, Allan."

He stared at her with a look of complete shock that quickly turned into one of utter joy. Then he swung her into his arms, spun her around once and let out a happy whoop. "You don't know how happy you've just made me."

"I'm the one who's happy," she told him.

He laughed. "This is the kind of argument I don't mind having. What do you say, Jane? The cast is all here—let's make it legal."

"Just like that?" Jane asked.

He put her down on her feet and took both her hands in his, swain style. "Will you marry me, Jane?"

Much as she would have liked to, just to prove that she was still her old sensible self, the Jane who always planned things out, she couldn't even pretend to hesitate. She was Jane the Spontaneous now. "I certainly will," she said, angling her lips to receive his celebratory kiss.

It was broken off by a moan in back of them, followed by a heavy thump. Jane looked up, startled, afraid her father might have passed out again from all the excitement. But this time it was Patricia who had fainted.

Grady dived to her side. "Somebody get a doctor!"

Dr. McGillicutty, quick from all this practice, scurried forward, black bag in hand.

After a few minutes, Patricia came to. She looked up into Grady's eyes and sighed. "Oh, Grady—thank goodness you're here. A man with good sense!"

"Me?" Grady asked, startled.

"Of course," Patricia cooed. "I've always said so."

Grady puffed up proudly. "Mostly it's just having the right instincts—and I've got 'em in spades, Patricia." He winked, then looked up for confirmation to the short man hovering over him. "Isn't that right, Dr. Winkel?"

Dr. Winkel nodded, and Grady covertly shot the man a questioning glance, as if to ask the good doctor what he thought of *this* woman.

Dr. Winkel sent him a curt nod.

Grady smiled and turned back to Patricia. "How are you feeling, sweetheart?"

Somehow, seeing Patricia surrounded by medical personnel from two different fields and Grady there to help her made Jane feel a little better. Maybe for once the two of them would be able to avoid physical disaster for long enough to figure out that they were a match made in financial heaven.

She turned back to Allan. "I'm so glad you remembered. I was going to have the hardest time explaining it all to you."

He smiled, and pulled her close. "I still might need a few details filled in here and there."

"I'll bet. Like me thinking Patricia was having your baby?"

Allan's eyes widened. "Apparently there are more details than I had thought."

But none of those details seemed to matter when, ten minutes later, the minister started speaking the words that would join them together forever. Though it had been delayed for a few weeks, the wedding came off beautifully. Jane's dress didn't feel quite so tight with Allan at her side and her breathing nearly back to normal. Aunt Katherine sang "Our Love Is Here to Stay" in near-perfect warble, and to Jane the words seemed suddenly very appropriate.

And when the bride and groom went to cut the cake, they discovered a brown-haired bride and groom again standing atop the partially eaten hundred-dollar cake, sneaked onto the third tier by a very happy, very robust Will, who didn't appear the least repentant for faking a heart attack and scaring Jane half to death—as long as it helped her land the right groom.

After he had the joy of watching his daughter shove

cake into Allan's mouth, and kiss her husband yet again, Will went out to the field to round up his prized cow. He even let her eat one of the sugared pansies in fond thanks for a job well done.

"Well, Zelda," he said as he walked her back onto his property. "If I do say so myself, I think we did okay. This place might liven up quite a bit now, with a grandchild on the way and the new dairy." He laughed. "And I guess new cows mean some company for you, too."

Zelda stared at him meaningfully as she munched on another sugared pansy, and in that moment, Will could have sworn that "some company" was what his pride and joy had in mind all along.

New York Times Bestselling Authors

JENNIFER BLAKE
JANET DAILEY
ELIZABETH GAGE

Three *New York Times* bestselling authors bring you three very sensuous, contemporary love stories—all centered around one magical night!

It is a warm, spring night and masquerading as legendary lovers, the elite of New Orleans society have come to celebrate the twenty-fifth anniversary of the Duchaise masquerade ball. But amidst the beauty, music and revelry, some of the world's most legendary lovers are in trouble....

Come midnight at this year's Duchaise ball, passion and scandal will be...

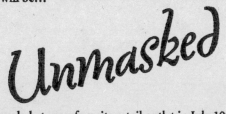

Unmasked

Revealed at your favorite retail outlet in July 1997.

HE SAID

♥

SHE SAID

Explore the mystery of male/female communication in this extraordinary new book from two of your favorite Harlequin authors.

Jasmine Cresswell and Margaret St. George bring you the exciting story of two romantic adversaries—each from their own point of view!

DEV'S STORY. CATHY'S STORY.
As he sees it. As she sees it.
Both sides of the story!

The heat is definitely on, and these two can't stay out of the kitchen!

Don't miss HE SAID, SHE SAID.
Available in July wherever Harlequin books are sold.

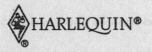

◆ HARLEQUIN®

And the Winner Is...
You!

...when you pick up these great titles
from our new promotion at your
favorite retail outlet this June!

Diana Palmer
The Case of the Mesmerizing Boss

Betty Neels
The Convenient Wife

Annette Broadrick
Irresistible

Emma Darcy
A Wedding to Remember

Rachel Lee
Lost Warriors

Marie Ferrarella
Father Goose

 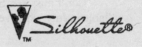

HARLEQUIN® Silhouette®

Look us up on-line at: http://www.romance.net   ATWI397-R

He changes diapers, mixes formula and
tells wonderful bedtime stories—he's

Mr. Mom

Three totally different stories of sexy, single
heroes each raising another man's child...
from three of your favorite authors:

MEMORIES OF THE PAST
by Carole Mortimer

THE MARRIAGE TICKET
by Sharon Brondos

TELL ME A STORY
by Dallas Schulze

Available this June wherever
Harlequin and Silhouette books are sold.

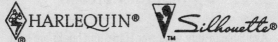

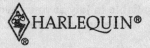